Y0-BDY-729

833.912 Kas
Kaschnitz.
Long shadows.

The Lorette Wilmot Library
Nazareth College of Rochester

Long Shadows
Stories by Marie Luise Kaschnitz

Long Shadows

LONG SHADOWS

Stories by
Marie Luise Kaschnitz

Translated and with a Foreword
by
Anni Whissen

CAMDEN HOUSE

WITHDRAWN
LORETTE WILMOT LIBRARY
NAZARETH COLLEGE

Translation of "Das dicke Kind" licensed by
Verlag Richard Scherpe.

Authorized translation of all other stories licensed by
Claassen Verlag (Krefeld).

Copyright © 1995 by
CAMDEN HOUSE, INC.

Published by Camden House, Inc.
Drawer 2025
Columbia, SC 29205 USA

Printed on acid-free paper.
Binding materials are chosen for strength and
durability

All Rights Reserved
Printed in the United Stated of America
First Edition

ISBN: 1-57113-021-7

Library of Congress Cataloging - in - Publication Data

Kaschnitz, Marie Luise, 1901-1974.
    [Lange Schatten. English]
    Long shadows : stories / by Marie Luise Kaschnitz ; translated and with
    a foreword by Anni Whissen.
    p.   cm. -- (Studies in German literature, linguistics, and culture)
    Includes bibliographical references.
    ISBN 1-57113-021-7 (alk. paper)
    I. Whissen, Anni. II. Title. III. Series: Studies in German literature, lin
    guistics, and culture (Unnumbered)
    PT2621.A73L313   1994
    833'. 912--dc20   94-24281
                                                           CIP

333.912
Kas

Acknowledgments

The translator wishes to express her thanks and appreciation to Wright State University for its generous support toward the publication of this book.

A. W.
October 1994

To Tom

Contents

Foreword

Marie Luise Kaschnitz (née von Holzing-Berstett) was born on January 31, 1901 in Karlsruhe, Germany. She grew up in Potsdam and Berlin, where her father pursued a military career as an army officer, ultimately attaining the rank of major general. Since her father was away a lot and her mother, a beautiful, fun-loving woman, was busily pursuing her own interests, Kaschnitz was raised, along with two older sisters and a younger brother, by a succession of nannies and governesses. The children were well provided for in this affluent, aristocratic household. They received a good education and were instilled with a clear sense of right and wrong. Yet something was amiss.

Kaschnitz's mother seemed to lack maternal warmth, and the relationship between Kaschnitz and her sisters was not close. Perhaps because her sisters were older, they stuck together and tended to exclude her from their activities. Consequently, she felt unwanted and insecure, even inferior. In addition, her parents' marriage was strained, especially after her father returned from the First World War in a state of deep depression. As a result Kaschnitz turned inward. Like Anne Frank, she created her own private world through diaries and journals, and as she recorded her thoughts throughout her life, she continued to sharpen her focus and refine her style.

In 1917 Kaschnitz went to Weimar to learn the book trade. Her apprenticeship there prepared her for the positions she held over the next few years, first in a publishing house in Munich and then in an antiquarian bookstore in Rome. In 1925 she married the Viennese archaeologist Guido von Kaschnitz-Weinberg, and three years later their only child, Iris Costanza, was born. Kaschnitz spent the first six years of her marriage in Rome, where her husband was affiliated with the German Archaeological Institute, but when he was offered a post at the university in Königsberg, the family returned to Germany. Two other university appointments followed, first in Marburg and then in Frankfurt. Having received no formal higher education herself, Kaschnitz enjoyed this connection with academic life, thriving on contacts with scholars from many different disciplines and benefiting from extended visits to Hungary, Yugoslavia, Italy, Greece, Turkey, and North Africa. When the German Archaeological Institute in Rome reopened after the Second World War, Guido became its director, and the Kaschnitzes moved back to Rome. They lived there from 1953 until 1956 when Guido was diagnosed as having a brain tumor and they were forced to return to Frankfurt.

Kaschnitz's literary career started in the thirties with two novels, *Liebe beginnt* (1933) and *Elissa* (1937). In the forties she published *Griechische Mythen* (1946), a personal and poetic retelling of select Greek myths, and *Gustave Courbet. Roman eines Malerlebens* (1949), a biography of the French painter. It was as a poet, however, that she finally gained recognition. Such lyrical volumes as *Totentanz und Gedichte zur Zeit* (1947), *Zukunftsmusik* (1950), and *Neue Gedichte* (1957) are among the most powerful commentaries to emerge from? post-war Germany. Her essays, *Engelsbrücke - Römische Betrachtungen* (1955), her short prose work *Das Haus der Kindheit* (1956), and her first volume of short stories *Lange Schatten* (1960) further enhanced her reputation.

When her husband died in 1958, Kaschnitz's world collapsed. The two had been very close, and the loss seemed unbearable. To ease the pain, she now devoted herself completely to her writing. Additional volumes of poetry such as *Dein Schweigen — meine Stimme* (1962) appeared in the following decade along with a collection of radio plays, *Hörspiele* (1962), autobiographical prose works such as *Wohin denn ich?* (1963), *Beschreibung eines Dorfes* (1966), and *Tage, Tage, Jahre* (1968), and collections of short stories, notably *Ferngespräche* (1966) and *Vogel Rock. Unheimliche Geschichten* (1969).

During her lifetime, Kaschnitz received several literary prizes. In 1955 she was awarded the Georg Büchner Prize, Germany's most prestigious prize for literature. The Immermann Prize followed in 1957, the Georg Mackensen Prize in 1964, and the Hebel Prize in 1970. Moreover, she was inducted into the *Ordre pour le mérite* and awarded an honorary doctorate from the University of Frankfurt.

During the 1960s Kaschnitz did a considerable amount of guest lecturing, first as poet-in-residence at the University of Frankfurt and later before audiences in Europe, South America, and the United States. Toward the end of her life, she spent much time in Rome, where she died on October 10, 1974. She is buried in the village of Bollschweil in the Black Forest, the seat of her parents' estate where she had spent her summers as a child and to which she returned again and again as an adult. Bollschweil, incidentally, is lovingly described in *Beschreibung eines Dorfes*, and the village made her an honorary citizen six years before her death.

The twenty-one stories presented here all explore various facets of the human condition, from the loneliness of childhood to the insecurity of adulthood and the vulnerability of old age. Many of them are journeys of self-discovery, journeys that parallel Kaschnitz's own life and reflect her thinking. Author and narrator are fused, and the personal story is altered through perspective, enhanced through imagination, and elevated through language. The stories explore the secret self, that part of the human being that is seldom revealed to others; and as her characters go about the task of discovering who they are or coming to terms with their lot, readers recognize events in their own lives that reveal who they are or where they stand.

According to Kaschnitz herself, all of her stories are about the way individual destinies, different as they may seem, are shaped by common feelings of loneliness, insecurity, even fear. The characters Kaschnitz writes about feel utterly alone in the world, whether they are children experiencing the pain of growing up or adults suffering the indignities of old age. In "The Fat Girl," Kaschnitz's most successful story and her personal favorite, a sensitive little girl must come to terms with who she really is. In "Long Shadows," high-spirited Rosie Walter, ordinarily so undaunted and self-assured, must get up the courage to fend off her Latin "suitor. " In "Home Alone," a lonely latchkey kid must learn to live without the "family" he has created. In these three stories, sensitive young adults experience rites of passage that give them the strength to go it alone. Underneath their tough exterior lurks an acute loneliness. There is no one to turn to. And yet they all have a certain resilience that pulls them through.

Loss and anxiety are also dominant themes in stories about older people. In "Brother Benda" an Irish monk loses his sight, and in "Adventures of an Old Man" Herr Seume loses his ability to enjoy a normal meal. As both men lose their health and their faculties, they are compelled to depend on other people and to suffer ridicule and humiliation at their hands. In "Circe's Mountain" an older woman recently widowed realizes that no one, not even her own daughter, can begin to share her grief.

In some of the stories, anxiety, nervousness, or fear puts an unbearable strain on family relationships, resulting in the disaffection of individual family members. In "The Piece of Straw" a woman is torn by confused feelings of anxiety, jealousy, anger, and fear when she suspects her husband of having an affair. "Ghosts," too, deals with the torment of conflicting emotions. In "Christine" a marriage is strained because the husband feels guilty for not having prevented a little girl from being strangled, whereas in "Thaw" a husband and wife live in fear of being killed by their adopted son.

Kaschnitz's stories are usually told from a woman's point of view, and in most cases it is the women who possess an inner strength that enables them to overcome their fears and accept their fates with stoic determination. And it is the women who, when forced to decide between giving in or resisting, choose to fight back. "The Fat Girl," "A Noon Hour in Mid-June," and "Circe's Mountain" are all good examples of this type of courage, but perhaps the best example is "The Red Net," a story about a woman who helps Jewish families escape from Germany during the Second World War. After helping to rescue numerous families, she decides to call a halt to her activities, for the danger is increases dramatically, and she longs to return to a normal life with her two sons before it is too late. But she has one more job to do: she must rescue a little girl. In a fine story full of suspense, Kaschnitz describes the conflicting emotions of a woman so frightened by the extra risks involved in this last mission that she almost does not go through with it. But she does—with tragic consequences.

In spite of her preference for strong female characters, Kaschnitz cannot really be called a feminist writer or even a champion of the feminist cause. If she champions any cause at all, it is that of the individual and of that individual's ability to make a difference. She clearly admires those who have the courage of their convictions, those who dare to uphold principles of honor and tradition, those who are not afraid to go against the grain when their conscience tells them to and who do what they must do regardless of the risks involved.

A number of Kaschnitz's stories have something mysterious or supernatural about them. In "Ghosts" a married couple meets some young people who, as it turns out, are actually dead. In "The Black Lake" a body of water in an unspoiled area of Italy seems to take revenge on the people who try to settle along its shores. In "Brother Benda" a sudden wind springs up and frightens some young people who are mocking a monk. In "A Noon Hour in Mid-June," at the precise moment when a woman almost drowns off the coast of Italy, she is proclaimed dead by someone far away in Germany. In "The Everlasting Light" a church father is able to locate a long lost person by swinging a pendulum over a map. In "Foreign Territory" two brave French pilots, who have experienced every possible danger in the war, are suddenly terrified by mysterious shadows and sounds in a German forest.

Kaschnitz's lasting encounter with the world of classical antiquity, especially in Rome, left an indelible mark on her writing. Seven of the twenty-one stories in this collection are set in Italy, and this setting adds an interesting dimension to the tales. There are frequent references to Greek and Roman mythology, and her descriptions of everyday people and places are rendered with great precision and much affection. In "The Old Manor House," "The Black Lake," "Circe's Mountain," and parts of "Walks," Kaschnitz registers her dismay at man's assault on nature. She witnesses, for example, the rapid change in the old Appian Way from a path through the meadows to a paved highway for thousands of cars. She sees the unspoiled Italian countryside suddenly dotted with vacation homes and with hotels and restaurants for tourists. She makes palpable the bitter truth that as civilization leaves its mark, something precious is irretrievably lost.

The majority of Kaschnitz's stories are first-person narratives. Her language is straightforward, and she speaks to the reader as to a good friend with whom she wants to share something important: This is what I heard, this is what I saw, this is what I thought. Some of her stories, especially "Circe's Mountain" and "Walks," are quite personal and introspective, like entries in a diary or a journal. But the seemingly loose, rambling style is not as simple as it looks. Even casual scrutiny reveals that these entries, far from being the random musings of an amateur, are selected and arranged with great care. The long monologues, in fact, have a lyrical quality about them that reveals the touch of a poet whose manipulation of language and syntax is surprisingly fresh and original.

For Kaschnitz, writing is both discipline and therapy, a way out of the deepest depression and sorrow. Like Rilke's Malte Laurids Brigge, who "learned how to see," she records in detail everything she sees and hears. Inventing new words as she goes, her writing flows from her pen in a stream-of-consciousness style, frequently without standard punctuation. This "controlled improvisation" results in vivid, compelling descriptions of places and events and a consistently penetrating insight into the human psyche.

Because Kaschnitz explores multiple facets of the human condition, her stories are as relevant today as when they were written. She deals with many timely issues (What happens to children when both parents work? What are the risks in adopting a child?) as well as with issues of universal significance (What is it like to grow up? What is it like to grow old?). Kaschnitz does not provide answers to these questions or editorialize about the problems. With the restraint of the true artist, she is content simply to put herself into the mind of her characters and present them with such compassion that her stories point the way to a deeper appreciation of our common humanity.

Long Shadows

Boring, all of it boring—the hotel lobby, the dining room, the beach where her parents lie around in the sun and fall asleep with their mouths open, where they wake up, yawn, go for a swim, fifteen minutes in the morning and fifteen minutes in the afternoon, relentlessly together. She sees them from behind. Her father's legs are too thin, her mother's too fat, and she's got varicose veins. The water wakes them up, and they splash around like children. Rosie never goes swimming with her parents; she has to keep an eye on her sisters, who are still little but no longer nice. In fact, they are stupid brats who pour sand in your book or put jelly fishes on your bare back. It's awful to have a family; other people, too, have problems with their families; Rosie can see that quite clearly. The dark-skinned man with the gold chain, for example, the one she calls the shah, hangs around the bar instead of sitting under the umbrella with his family, or he races his motorboat, making wild turns at top speed, always by himself. It's a real pain to have a family. Why can't you be born already grown up and be on your own? I'm going out by myself, Rosie announces one day after lunch. And just to be on the safe side, she adds, to the village to buy postcards, picture postcards for my friends in school. Of course, she has no intention of sending postcards to those ninnies: greetings from the blue Mediterranean, how are you, I'm fine. We want to go along, her little sisters shout, but thank God they aren't allowed; they have to take their afternoon nap. All right, as long as you take the main road up to the market and then come right back, and don't talk to any strangers, says her father, his poor old office back hunched, as he trudges behind her mother and her little sisters. He was out in the boat this morning, but a sailor is about the last thing he'll ever be.

Just up the main road, you can see the village up above, its walls and towers hugging the mountainside, but her parents have not been up there yet. They said it was too far, too hot, which is actually not so far from the truth. There is no shade anywhere. Rosie doesn't need any shade. Why would she? She has covered herself with suntan lotion. She feels fine no matter where she is, as long as nobody tells her what to do or asks any questions. When you're alone, everything becomes big and strange and begins to belong to you: my street, my mangy black cat, my dead bird— it's gross, covered with ants but worth touching nonetheless, mine. My long legs in faded linen pants, my white sandals, one foot in front of the other, no one is on the road, the sun beats down. Where the road reaches the hillside, it starts to wind, a blue serpent in golden grapevines, and in the fields the crickets chirp like crazy. Rosie cuts through the gardens, an old woman comes toward her, a mummy. What's she doing running around like that when she should have been dead and buried long ago? A young man passes Rosie and then stops. Rosie's face tightens. The fellows around here are pretty pushy; you don't need parents to tell you that. What do you need parents for anyway? What they can tell you changed long ago. No thanks, I don't need any company, Rosie says politely as she walks past the young man the way she has seen the local girls doing—back straight, spine rigid, chin down, eyes lowered and unfriendly. He contents himself with some flattering remarks, which sound utterly stupid to Rosie's ear. Vineyards, cascades of pink geraniums, nut trees, acacia trees, vegetable beds, white houses, pink houses. Her palms are sweaty, and perspiration runs down her face. Finally she reaches the summit, then the town. Rosie gets wind in her sails and floats happily through dark alleys, past fruit stands and flat tin boxes filled with colorful, glistening, round-eyed fish. My market, my town, my shop with its multitudes of rubber animals and its firmament of straw hats, not to mention stands full of postcards, from which Rosie picks out three with gaudy-blue ocean panoramas just for the heck of it.

Farther down the square, no oh-ing or ah-ing over the castle and the church facades, but instead curious glances at the modest window displays and into the ground-floor bedrooms with their sentimental pictures of the Virgin hanging above ornate cast iron bedsteads. The streets are almost deserted during this early afternoon hour. A mangy little dog of indeterminate breed barks at a boy who is standing by a window making faces at it. In her pants pocket Rosie finds half a roll left over from breakfast. Catch, you little mongrel, she says, holding it out to the dog, and the dog dances around her like a trained monkey. Rosie throws out the roll and immediately retrieves it. This ugly little thing hopping around on its hind legs makes her laugh, and she finally sits down on the curb and scratches its dirty white belly. "Hey," the boy calls down from the window, and Rosie calls back "Hey." Their voices re-echo, and for a moment it is as if they are the only two persons who are awake in this hot drowsy town. The girl is pleased when the dog follows her as she walks on; just to have company without being asked questions, to be able to talk, come doggy, now we'll walk out the gate. This gate is not the same one Rosie walked through on her way into town, and the road definitely doesn't lead down to the beach. Instead it goes up the mountain, cutting through an oak forest and then winding along the fertile slope with a full view of the ocean. Her parents had planned to go on a hike up there and then on to the lighthouse. It's good to know they are lying down now in their darkened room at the foot of the mountain.

Rosie is in another world: my olive grove, my orange tree, my ocean, my little dog, fetch the stone. The dog fetches it and barks at the dark blue strip of melting asphalt, and now it runs back a little way toward town. At this point someone comes around the bend, a boy, the boy who was standing by the window making faces, a sturdy, sunburned fellow. Your dog? Rosie asks, and the boy nods, comes closer, and starts to point out the sights. At first Rosie, who knows a little Italian from a stay in the Tessin, is happy, but then she's disappointed since she had already figured out that the ocean is the ocean, the mountain the mountain, and the islands the islands. She walks faster, but the stocky boy stays right on her heels and keeps chattering away. Everything he points to with his short brown fingers loses its magic. What remains is a postcard like the ones Rosie bought, gaudy-blue and poison-green. I wish he would go away and take his dog with him, she thinks, and suddenly she is tired of the dog, too. She stops when she sees ahead of her a trail branching off to the left and leading steeply downhill between the cliff and the woodland. Then she gets out the few coins left over from her purchase, thanks the boy, and sends him away, forgetting about him right away and enjoying this adventure, this rocky trail, which soon gets lost in the thicket.

Rosie has forgotten all about her parents and her sisters. She has even forgotten herself as a person, with a name and an age, the school girl Rosie Walter, 7th grade, who isn't applying herself. Enough said, a free spirit, in her own defiant way in love with the sun, the salt air, her freedom, an adult like the shah. Too bad he doesn't go for walks; otherwise they could meet here and watch for ships passing on the horizon without any stupid chitchat.

The trail turns into steps that wind around the cliff. Rosie sits down on a step. She touches the fissured rock with all ten fingers. She smells the mint, which she crumbles between her palms. The sun burns, the ocean shimmers, and Pan sits on the broom-covered hillside. But there are gaps in Rosie's education; she never heard of him. Pan is stalking his nymph, but Rosie sees only the boy, twelve years old. For cryin' out loud, there he is again. She's really annoyed. He leaps down the rocky steps on silent dusty-gray feet, this time without his dog. What do you want? Go home, says Rosie, wanting to follow the path that runs along the cliff for a while, at this point without any railing at all. Down there is the abyss and the sea. The boy doesn't repeat his "ecco il mare, ecco l'isola" anymore, but he doesn't leave either. Instead he follows her, now uttering a strange, almost pleading sound, which has something inhuman about it and which frightens Rosie. What's with him? What's he up to? she thinks. She wasn't born

3

yesterday, but surely that can't be it. He's only twelve years old, a mere child. Of course, the boy might have gotten ideas in his head from his older friends, his big brothers. There is always talk in the village, constant whispering about the foreign girls who'll do anything for love and who walk through the vineyards and the olive groves by themselves. No husband or brother is going to pull out a gun, and the magic word "amore, amore" brings tears to their eyes and results in kisses. That is autumn talk, winter talk, in the cold dim café or on the wet, gray, deserted beach, talk that rekindles the glow of summer. Just you wait, my friend; in two or three years there'll be someone for you, too. She'll be coming across the square, you'll be standing by the window, and she'll smile at you. Then you just run after her, my friend, don't be shy, go ahead and touch her. What? She doesn't want to? But she is only pretending; she wants to all right.

Not that the boy, the master of the little monkey-like dog, would have remembered advice like that at this particular moment, remembered the great love song and summer song of winter. Further, the two or three years are by no means up. He is still Peppino, the little snotnose whose mother slaps him whenever he snitches jam from the pot. He can't swagger like the older boys, can't wave and shout "ah, bella," now that he wants to try his luck with this girl, the first one that smiled at him and lured his dog away. His luck, he doesn't know what that is, grown-up talk and innuendo, or does he suddenly know after all what it is all about as Rosie moves away from him, pushing his hand away and, her face all white, flattening herself against the cliff? He knows all right, and because he cannot demand it, he begins to beg and plead in a language he thinks strangers will understand, a language that consists only of infinitives: come please, please hug, please kiss please, love please, all of these uttered very quickly with trembly voice and lips, saliva dribbling from his mouth.

When Rosie laughs nervously and says: Don't be ridiculous, what are you thinking of? How old are you anyway? he moves away and before her eyes jumps out of his adolescent skin, so to speak, getting angry wrinkles in his forehead and a wild greedy expression on his face. He'd better not touch me, he'd better not hurt me, Rosie thinks, as she looks around in vain for help. But the road lies high above beyond the cliff, there is no human being in sight on the zigzag trail at her feet, and by the ocean down below the noise of the surf is sure to drown out any scream. Down there by the sea her parents are having their second swim now. I wonder where Rosie is? She was just going to buy postcards for her friends at school. Oh, the classroom, so wonderfully dark in November. What a nice job you did, Rosie, on that drawing of yours of the bluejay wing. We'll have to put it in the display case for everyone to see. Rosie Walter and a cross by her name, your dear classmate, dead by the blue Mediterranean, we had better not say how. Ridiculous, Rosie thinks, trying once more with clumsy words to talk some sense into the boy, but at this point a larger vocabulary would have been of no use either. Young Pan, pleading, stammering, glowing, must have his nymph. Tearing off his shirt and pants, he suddenly stands naked on the gray-hot rocky soil in front of the yellow bush. It is deathly quiet now, and from down below you can hear the roar of the indifferent sea.

Staring at the naked boy, Rosie forgets her fear, so beautiful does his sunburned body suddenly seem to her—the band of white skin left by his bathing trunks, the crown of yellow flowers around his damp black hair. But now he steps out of his golden halo and comes toward her, baring his white fangs. Suddenly he is the wolf from the fairy tale, a wild beast. You can defend yourself against animals. Rosie's own narrow-chested father once proved that, but Rosie was still very young then. She had forgotten all about that, but now she remembers again. No, Rosie, not a stone; you just look a dog straight in the eye. Okay now, let it come closer, don't blink. You see? It's trembling, it's crouching, it's running away. That boy is a stinking cur, it has eaten carrion, maybe it has rabies, stand very still now. I can do that, too, Dad. Rosie, who is cowering against the side of the cliff like a bundle of misery, straightens up, grows tall, rises from her child's shoulders and stares angrily and fixedly at the boy for several seconds without blinking or moving a muscle. It is still terribly quiet, and suddenly there is an overwhelming fragrance from thousands of inconspicuous macchia flowers, sweet as honey and bitter as herbs. And in that stillness and fragrance the boy really does collapse like a doll whose sawdust is running out.

It's hard to understand what happened. You can only imagine that Rosie's gaze must have been terrifying. There must have been some primitive force in it, some primitive defense mechanism, just as the boy's pleading and stammering and last wild gesture contained the primitive force of desire. Everything new, everything newly awakened in these children on that hot shimmering afternoon, a brand-new experience, love of life, desire, and shame; a rite of spring, but without love, only longing and fear. Ashamed of himself the boy retreats under Rosie's stony stare, step by step, whimpering like a sick infant. Rosie, too, feels ashamed of the effect of this gaze of hers, which she will never find the courage to repeat, not even in front of a mirror. Finally the boy, who has turned around quickly with his clothes in his hands and silently run up the rocky ladder, sits on the wall buttoning up his shirt and mumbling to himself, angry and blind with tears. The little dog is there again, too, barking its bold and carefree bark. Rosie runs down the zigzag trail wanting to feel relieved that she got

5

away. Fathers, I tell you! I guess you can learn a thing or two from your father after all. But deep down she feels unhappy as she stumbles, blind with tears, between spurge and white thornbushes. Your classmate Rosie! You went all the way to Italy, I hear. Yes, thanks, it was wonderful. Wonderful and terrifying, that's what it was. When she has finally reached the beach, Rosie washes her face and neck with sea water and thinks: There's no way I'm going to tell, not one word. Then she strolls along the edge of the shore to the bathing beach and her parents, while the boy slowly trots home on the road above. And so much time has passed with all this that the sun is already slanting across the mountain so that both Rosie and the boy cast long shadows as they walk. They are long, widely separated shadows, over the tops of the young piñons on the slope and over the sea, which is much paler now.

Ghosts

If I ever experienced a ghost story firsthand? Sure, I did—in fact, I still remember it well, and I'll tell you all about it. But when I'm done, promise not to ask any questions or demand any explanation, because I know only what I'm about to tell you and nothing more.

The experience I have in mind began in a theater, in the Old Vic in London actually, at a performance of Shakespeare's *Richard II*. My husband and I were in London for the first time then, and the city made a tremendous impression on us. After all, we were used to living in the country, in Austria, and we were familiar with Vienna, of course, as well as with Munich and Rome, but we didn't know what a real metropolis was. I remember we were no sooner on our way to the theater when we got into a strange mood of excitement and happiness as we rode up and down the steep escalators to the subway and chased after trains in the icy tunnel winds on the platforms. Eventually we were sitting in front of the curtain, still closed, like children who are seeing a Christmas fairy tale on the stage for the first time. Finally the curtain rose, and the play began. Soon the young king appeared, a handsome fellow, a playboy, but someone about whom we knew what destiny had in store for him, how it would warp him, and how he would finally perish, done in by his own decision. I was completely absorbed in the action from the start and never took my eyes off the stage, so captivated was I by the shimmering colors of the sets and the costumes. Anton, however, seemed preoccupied and distracted, as if something else had suddenly caught his attention. When I turned to him at one point looking to see if he was enjoying the play as much as I was, I noticed he wasn't watching the stage at all and that he was barely listening to what was being said. Instead he seemed to be staring at a woman who was sitting in the row in front of us, a little farther to the right. The woman turned halfway toward him a few times, too, something like a timid smile appearing whenever I could see more than just her profile.

Anton and I had been married six years at that time, and I had learned by then that he liked to look at pretty women and young girls. He also enjoyed approaching them in order to test the magnetism of his beautifully shaped southern European eyes. This attitude had never given rise to any real jealousy on my part, and I wasn't jealous now either, just a little annoyed that because of this pastime of his Anton was missing what to me was so well worth experiencing. For that reason I didn't pay any further attention to the conquest he was trying to make. Even when he lightly touched my arm once during the first act and motioned in the woman's direction by raising his chin and lowering his eyelids, I just nodded amiably and turned my attention to the stage again. During the intermission, however, there was no getting away from the problem any longer. As quickly as he could, Anton elbowed his way ahead, pulling me with him to the exit, and I realized that he was prepared to wait there until the stranger walked past us; that is, if she was even planning to leave her seat. At first she didn't make any preparation to do so, and, in fact, it turned out that she was not alone but in the company of a young man who like herself had a delicate, pale complexion and reddish blond hair and who made a weary, almost lifeless impression. There's nothing particularly pretty about her, I thought, nor is she especially elegant in her pleated skirt and sweater, as if she were dressed for a hike in the country. And then I suggested that we go out in the lobby, and I started talking about the play, although I could feel there was no point in it at all. For Anton didn't come with me, nor did he listen to me. He stared almost rudely over at the young people, who were getting up now and moving toward us, but in a strangely slow motion, almost as if in a trance. He simply can't start talking to them, I thought. That isn't done here, that's not done anywhere, but here in this country it's an unpardonable offense. In the meantime the girl walked right past us without looking at us. Her program slipped out of her hand and floated down on the carpet, the way a lace handkerchief might have at one time, suivez-moi, an echo from the distant past. Anton stooped down to pick up the glossy brochure, but instead of handing it back, he asked if he might have a look at it. He went ahead and did just that while mumbling all kinds of nonsense about the performance and the actors in his poor English, and finally he introduced himself and me to the strangers, which seemed to surprise the young man quite a bit. Indeed, the young girl's face showed both surprise and resistance, even though she apparently had fully intended to drop her program and was now looking into my husband's eyes quite openly. Yet her gaze was at the same time wistful and sad. She ignored the hand that Anton had innocently stretched out in continental fashion, and she didn't give her name but said merely: We're brother and sister. The sound of her voice, which was unusually delicate and sweet and nothing to be afraid of at all, somehow made my flesh crawl. At these words, which made Anton blush like a schoolboy, we started moving. We walked around the lobby and talked haltingly about this, that, and the other, and whenever we passed the mirrors, the strange girl would stop and pull at her hair while smiling encouragingly at Anton in the mirror. Then the bell sounded. We went back to our seats, and I listened and watched and forgot about the English couple.

But Anton didn't forget about them. He didn't look over at them so frequently anymore, but I felt he was merely waiting for the play to be over and that he didn't take the terrible and lonely death of the aged king to heart at all. When the curtain fell, he didn't wait for the applause and the curtain calls at all but rushed over to the couple, urging them and apparently persuading them to give him their coat checks. Then with an agility utterly strange and unpleasant, he immediately pushed and shoved his way through the patiently waiting audience only to return a moment later loaded down with coats and hats. I was annoyed at his eagerness and convinced that in the end we would be icily dismissed by our new acquaintances and that after the emotional effect the play had had on me I would have no choice but to go home with my disappointed and ill-tempered Anton.

But it all turned out quite differently, because when we had put our coats on and stepped outside, it was raining hard. There was hardly a taxi to be had, but with a lot of running and waving Anton finally managed to round one up, and the four of us squeezed into it in such high spirits that I forgot I was out of sorts. Where to? Anton asked. And the girl said in her bright, sweet voice: To our place. She gave the chauffeur her address and to my great surprise invited us up for a cup of tea. My name is Vivian, she said, and my brother's name is Laurie, and let's just use our first names. I looked askance at the girl and was surprised at how much more lively she had become, as if she had been paralyzed before and was just now—in our or in Anton's physical presence—able to move her limbs. When we got out, Anton rushed to pay the driver, and I stood there looking at the houses, which were butted right up against each other and all completely alike, narrow with small temple-like porches and with front yards containing similar plants. It crossed my mind that it would be pretty difficult to find any house here again, and I was almost happy to spot something unique in these people's garden after all: a sitting stone cat. In the meantime Laurie had opened the front door, and now he and his sister led us up the stairs. Anton used the opportunity to whisper to me: I know her, I'm sure I know her, if only I knew from where. Once upstairs, Vivian immediately disappeared to heat the water for the tea, and Anton asked her brother if the two had been abroad recently and, if so, where. Laurie answered reluctantly, almost distressed. I couldn't tell if the personal question offended him or if he couldn't remember. It almost seemed that way, for he ran his hand across his forehead a couple of times and looked unhappy. There's something not quite right about him, I thought. Nothing is quite right here: a strange house, so quiet and dark and the furniture covered with dust as if the place hadn't been lived in for the longest time. Even the light bulbs in the lamps were burned out or had been unscrewed. Candles, many of which were standing in tall silver candelabra on the old furniture, had to be lit. That actually looked pretty nice and added to the conviviality. The cups, which Vivian brought in on a glass tray, were beautiful, too; delicate with a lovely blue pattern, entire dreamscapes could be seen on the china. The tea was strong and tasted bitter, and there was no sugar and cream to go with it. What are you talking about? Vivian asked, looking at Anton, and my husband repeated his questions with an almost impolite urgency. Yes, Vivian answered quickly, we were in Austria, in … But now she, too, couldn't remember the name of the place. Confused, she stared at the round table, which was covered with a fine layer of dust.

At that point, Anton got out his cigarette case, a flat, gold case that he had inherited from his father and still used, contrary to the prevailing custom of offering cigarettes out of the pack. He opened it and offered each of us one, and then he closed it again and put it on the table, something I remembered clearly the next morning when he couldn't find it.

In any case, we drank tea and smoked. Then Vivian suddenly got up and turned on the radio, and above all kinds of twanging snatches of sound and voices the noise over the loudspeaker softly changed to jingling dance music. Let's dance, Vivian said, looking at my husband, and Anton immediately got up and put his arm around her waist. Her brother made no effort to ask me to dance, so we stayed at the table listening to the music and watching the couple move back and forth at one end of the large room. So English women are not that reserved, I thought, already aware that I meant something else, because just like before, a coolness, a gracious gentle coolness, emanated from the strange girl. At the same time, however, there was also a strange greed about her, as her small hands clung to my husband's shoulders like the tendrils of a climbing plant and her lips moved silently as if they were uttering cries of the most dire agony and distress. Anton, who was still a vigorous young man and a good dancer at that time, didn't seem to be aware that there was anything unusual about his dancing partner's behavior. He looked serenely and lovingly down at her, and sometimes he looked over at me in the same way, as if he wanted to say: Don't think anything about it, it'll pass, it's nothing. But although Vivian, so delicate and slender, moved about with him, this dance, which didn't end as radio music normally does but merely changed rhythm and melody, seemed to put an immense strain on him. His forehead was soon covered with beads of perspiration, and when he and Vivian passed right by me once, his breathing sounded almost like panting or gasping. Laurie, who sat drowsily next to me, suddenly started beating in time with the music, sometimes skillfully using his knuckles and sometimes the teaspoon as well as tapping my husband's cigarette case on the table. All of this lent a breathless urgency to the music, which suddenly frightened me. A trap, I thought. They have lured us up here, and we'll be robbed or dragged off. And right afterward: What a crazy thought. Who are we anyway? Insignificant foreigners, tourists, theatergoers who carry nothing on our persons except a little money, possibly to go get something to eat after the performance. Suddenly I got very sleepy. I tried to stifle a yawn a couple of times. Hadn't the tea we had been drinking been exceptionally bitter, and hadn't Vivian brought in the cups already poured so that a sleeping pill might well have been dissolved in ours and not in the ones that the English couple were drinking out of? Let's get out of here, I thought. Let's get back to the hotel. I tried to get my husband's attention again, but he wasn't looking in my direction. His eyes were closed now, the delicate face of his dancing partner resting on his shoulder.

Where's the phone? I asked brusquely. I'd like to call a cab. Accommodatingly Laurie reached behind him. The unit was sitting on a trunk, but when Laurie picked up the receiver, there was no dial tone. Laurie merely shrugged apologetically, but Anton's attention had been aroused now. He stopped and pulled away from the girl, who looked up at him, surprised while teetering dangerously like a fragile flower in the wind. It's late, my husband said. I'm afraid we've got to go now. To my surprise the couple made no objection. A few friendly and polite remarks were exchanged: Thank you for a lovely evening and so on. Then the laconic Laurie showed us down the stairs to the front door while Vivian remained on the landing upstairs, leaning over the banister and uttering little birdlike sounds which could mean anything or nothing at all.

There was a taxi stand nearby, but Anton wanted to walk part of the way. At first he was quiet and seemed exhausted, but then he suddenly started talking a mile a minute. He said he was sure he had seen the sister and brother somewhere before and not too long ago either, probably in Kitzbühel last spring; after all, that was a pretty difficult name for a foreigner to remember. No wonder Vivian hadn't been able to think of it. He said he remembered a specific incident now. He had thought of it just before, while dancing with Vivian: a mountain road, glancing back and forth from car to car. He had been alone in his, and in another, a red sports car, had been the sister and brother with the girl at the wheel, and after a short traffic jam when he was driving next to them for a minute, the car had passed him and taken off like a rocket. Didn't I think she was pretty and something special, Anton asked right afterward. I said she was pretty all right and something special, too, but kind of spooky; and I reminded him of the musty smell in the apartment and of the dust and the disconnected phone. Anton had not noticed any of this, nor did he want to hear about it now. But we were in no mood to argue, just very tired, and so we stopped talking after a while and went back to our hotel in peace and went to bed.

We had planned to spend the next morning at the Tate Gallery. In fact, we already had a catalog for this famous collection of paintings, and over breakfast we were leafing through it and trying to make up our minds which paintings to see and which ones not to. But right after breakfast my husband noticed his cigarette case was missing, and when I reminded him that the last I had seen of it was on the table at the English couple's place, he suggested we go and pick it up before our visit to the museum. I was sure he had left it there on purpose, but I didn't say anything. We found the street on the city map, and then we took the bus to a square nearby. It wasn't raining any more. A pale golden early autumn mist hovered over the broad park lawns, and large buildings with columns and gables emerged and disappeared again mysteriously in the swirling mist.

Anton was in a great mood, and so was I. I had forgotten all about the anxiety of last night and was eager to see what our new friends would look and act like in the light of day. We had no trouble finding the street and the house, but we were surprised to see all the shutters lowered, as if everything were asleep or the inhabitants had gone off on an extended trip. Since nothing stirred after my first reluctant ring, we pressed the bell harder, finally almost discourteously long and loud. There was also an old-fashioned brass knocker on the door, and this, too, we finally made use of, but we still didn't hear steps inside or voices approaching. We finally left, but just a few houses down the street Anton stopped again. It wasn't so much because of the cigarette case, he said, but something could have happened to the young people, gas poisoning, for example. There were gas fireplaces everywhere around here, and he had seen one in their room, too. He didn't want to believe for a moment that the two might have taken off. In any case, the police would have to be notified, and besides he was in no frame of mind to go looking at paintings in a museum. In the meantime the fog had lifted. A beautiful blue autumn sky could be seen above the quiet street and above house number 79 which, now that we were coming back, was sitting there just as still and as lifeless as before.

The neighbors, I said. We've got to check with the neighbors. Just then a window opened in the house next door on the right, and a heavy-set woman shook her mop over the pretty fall asters in the front yard. We called to her and tried to make ourselves understood. We didn't have a last name to go by, only Vivian and Laurie, but the woman seemed to know right away whom we meant. She retrieved her mop, then leaned out the window, her large bosom in its flowery blouse pressing against the sill, and looked down at us frightened. We were here in this house just last night,

Anton said. We left something that we would like to pick up. The woman suddenly looked suspicious. That was impossible, she said in a shrill voice. She was the only one with a key, and the house was empty. Since when? I asked automatically, already thinking we had made a mistake in the house number, although the stone cat was there in the front yard, now in bright sunshine.

It's been three months since the young people passed away, the woman said quite emphatically. Passed away? we asked, starting to talk at the same time. Can't be. We were with them last night at the theater, we had tea with them, we listened to music and danced.

Just a moment, the heavy-set woman said, slamming the window shut. I was sure she would call now and have us hauled away, to the insane asylum or the police station. But she came down to the street right away with a curious look on her face and a big bunch of keys in her hand. Don't you tell me I'm crazy, she said; I know what I'm talking about. The young people are dead and buried. They took their car abroad and broke their necks over there, in the mountains somewhere, with this crazy fast driving of theirs.

In Kitzbühel? my husband asked upset. The woman said that might indeed have been the name of the place, but then again it could have been something else; nobody ever could understand these foreign names. Nevertheless, she was already charging ahead of us, up the stairs, opening the door just so we could see for ourselves that she was telling the truth and that the house was indeed empty. As far as she was concerned, we should feel free to go through the apartment, but she wouldn't be able to turn the lights on. She had removed the light bulbs for her own use, the manager had had no objection.

We followed the woman. It smelled damp and musty, and on the stairs I took my husband's hand and said it must simply be a completely different street, or we had just dreamed the whole thing. It was entirely possible for two people to have the same dream in the same night; things like that did happen, and now it was time to get out of there. Of course, Anton said relieved; you're quite right. What are we doing here anyway? And he stopped and reached in his pocket to get out some money that he wanted to give the neighbor lady for her trouble. But she had already slipped away and gone into the apartment upstairs. We had to catch up with her and go in there, too, although we no longer felt like it and were quite certain the whole thing was a case of mistaken identity or a figment of our imagination. Come on in, the woman said, starting to raise one of the shutters, not completely, just part way, enough so that we could clearly recognize all the furniture, especially a round table with chairs around it and a fine layer of dust on the top. On the table there was only a single item, which glistened now that the sun hit it: a flat gold cigarette case.

The Red Net

In loving memory of Marie Louise Hensel

I'm sure it wasn't really like that, but it might have been the way it was that warm, hazy July afternoon by the lake. Vacationers were on their way to this inn or the other for afternoon coffee. Did you know you can get cake over there without bread coupons? And they give you a great big piece. For those were still the days when bread coupons were a must and when you had to walk to get places. Here, of course, you were close to the border, and it disappeared at Lake Constance. Out on the lake there were fishermen, and sometimes they would even sail across the lake and bring something back or take something along with them, like live cargo. A human being with his heart in his throat among the passengers, someone who would crouch anxiously whenever the search light came closer. His money would lie hidden under the milk cup in the fishermen's hut on the home shore, quite a bit of money. After all, the ferryman was risking something, too: his freedom, maybe even his head. In this beautiful scenery, therefore, there was along with the hushed conversation over the cup of real coffee and the piece of cake you could get without coupons yet another conversation, a quieter one, a more dangerous one: cautious directions; yes, the fellow over there by the mill behind us; yes, the fellow out there on the point in front of us, under the tall silver poplar, he is into that sort of thing.

It's a warm, hazy summer afternoon. A woman is taking a walk: gray skirt, black cardigan, sturdy shoes. Black hair, but nothing foreign about her, certainly nothing Jewish, North German pronunciation and a flat low-German face. No Biblical first name on her passport, no yellow star on her chest. When you look like that, you don't need to avoid your friends or go for walks by yourself. Indeed, Renata wasn't alone either. A woman from her hotel, the wife of some district judge or other, was with her. The two women walked together, not slowly, but not fast either, under the apple trees which promised a lot of fruit. The district judge's wife with her fat, pink cheeks bent down once in a while to pick a scabiosa or a daisy or a sorrel flower growing in the meadow, and soon she was holding a pretty bouquet in her hand.

"Have you heard from your son?" she asked. Renata said yes, thank you, he is in the middle zone of operations now, but not quite at the front; he's fine. Her little boy was fine, too, she said; he was still in school, at a boarding school in Northern Germany far away from here. The district judge's wife wanted to know if the boy might be coming down on vacation, and Renata said, sure, maybe even next Sunday. He was a big boy now; soon he would be taller than she. And was Renata maybe a widow? the woman wanted to know. Renata said yes, but not a war widow. Her husband had had a bad heart and had suddenly collapsed when he was only forty years old, three years before the war. This conversation is inane, Renata thought, but it's better not to walk by yourself. That way you don't arouse so much suspicion. If anyone should ask the district judge's wife about me later on, she would say we had gone for a walk together and that we had gone begging for food, a pound of butter, a jar of honey. Who didn't? Very soon, in five or ten minutes, Renata would suggest that they do just that. They could try the farm houses, couldn't they, for your boy and mine. But not together, of course; if there are two of you, they never give you anything.

When they had gotten a little father past the hill, they could already see the house on the point, the one with the tall poplar in front. But first one had to go along the hill, the path got narrower, how high the grass was already. In the high grass the two women ran into a family walking nicely single file, for who would dare set foot on the meadow? The farmers would attack the invaders with raised scythes. Three persons were coming toward them. Renata walked past the woman without really looking at her, but she did take a good look at the man. He really wasn't a hiker at all, but a homebody with awkward movements, someone who seemed deeply unhappy as he dragged the whimpering child behind him. My family, Renata thought, my child, and that could easily have been the case, for what was in the envelope hidden in her bra? Only a name, numbers, a date, but no picture. She stopped and looked after the people. The child was a girl of about six. She turned around now, with her impish grin and made a gesture with her hand that suggested she wanted to pull Renata down in the high grass so that they could play, keeping their bodies low, a sinister little game.

"I guess they need it, too," the district judge's wife said in motherly fashion, meaning by that the nights without air raid sirens, the sandwiches, the fresh air. Renata walked a little faster. Yes, she thought, they need it all right, this last walk together, this final parting, but you can't ask, you can't turn around one more time. If all goes well, the child will be in Switzerland tonight. If all goes well? Why shouldn't it go well? She had the correct address. Under the tall poplar you could already see the shimmering waves of the lake. Another farm lay to the left, high above the road.

"You try up there, if that's all right with you; I'll try down there in the house with the poplar tree. Whatever we get, we'll share." This was fine with the district judge's wife; she was ready for action. Begging for food may not be the most pleasant thing, but it's an exciting adventure nonetheless, and what a delight it is to come home with a couple of eggs and a bag full of flour.

When Renata, alone now, started down the path leading to the lake, she saw not far from the house with the poplar tree and also on the lake shore yet another fisherman's cottage or farmer's house lying as if bewitched behind elder bushes and wild rose hedges. That would be the place to live, she thought. The fog comes across the lake; you wouldn't hear a thing, you wouldn't see a thing. As she headed for the silver poplar, she kept staring at the other house, strangely excited, as if this particular house were her real destination, as if this spot were the place where she would fulfill her life. She was suddenly sorry she had to be so careful and didn't dare speak to anyone about herself, even to the district judge's wife, who seemed to be a good-natured person. I don't care about butter, she would have liked to say. What I have in mind is something else. I have built on the destiny of the Jews. She liked this expression; you could imagine something like a house above an abyss, and down below, the stream roared, turbid gurgling water carrying lots of debris, tree trunks, and splintered beams, not to mention human beings, alive, stretching out their arms and crying for help. And I myself was outside of this on a safe shore, able to haul someone out here and there because I didn't arouse suspicion, an Arian, the mother of a soldier, and well off at that.

This is more or less what Renata would have liked to say. Maybe she even wanted to tell what all had been asked of her in this regard and what she could have accomplished with a clear head and defiant temperament, even without fear; but today she was a little weary and longed for peace and happiness. The district judge's wife was already over there on the slope, and you probably couldn't trust her either. After all, whom could you trust these days? Even the people in the house with the poplar tree, which Renata had almost reached by now, couldn't be told the truth right away. You had to feel your way around, ask for food or lodging. A woman was just coming out of the house. She called her dog, which had been barking for quite a while and was pulling at its chain. When Renata went up to her and asked for a room, the woman looked at her anxiously and said she didn't have any, nor did she have any butter or milk and, for God's sake, would Renata please go away. This expression "for God's sake" might have puzzled Renata, but she was already in full swing, seeing the boats and nets and, on the other side of the dull, blue surface, the foreign shore, beautiful and serene. She simply had to speak to the woman's husband, she said; she was bringing him greetings and had matters to discuss with him. The woman, a tall heavy person, looked at Renata the whole time, distressed and sad.

"Come along, then," she finally said, leading Renata into a room on the ground floor, a kind of parlor with a table and chairs around it and an ugly sideboard and strange green shadows, as if mold were permeating the wall. Then she left the room to go looking for her husband, and Renata sat down at the table, got a stack of bills out of her shoulder bag, and kept them in her hand. The grandfather clock uttered an ugly, screeching sound and struck four times, and through the gray muslin curtain Renata could see how one of the cows out there in the apple orchard arched its back and relieved itself. After a while the fisherman came into the room, a short fellow with whitish-blond hair, weak fish eyes, and a sweaty face.

"What do you want? Who sent you?" he asked hostilely. He didn't sit down but just rested his little whitish-blue fists on the table, which was covered with a silky cloth with a fringe. Renata was suddenly on her guard.

"Never mind who sent me or where I got my information," she said, "but I do know you do this sort of thing."

"Do what?" the man asked angrily. "I'm not doing anything I shouldn't be, lady; you've got that all wrong." And Renata actually thought she had the wrong house and casually moved her hand with the money down in her lap.

"I wanted to rent a room," she said. "Any law against that?" she said looking at the fisherman and laughing.

"Don't tell me you came to rent a room," the man said sternly, blinking in the direction of the door, where someone apparently was motioning to him.

"All right," said Renata looking him right in the eye. "I didn't come here to rent a room. I wanted to pay for a ride, but if you don't want the job, maybe you can give me the name of someone who does."

The man didn't answer. His eyes were still fixed at the door behind Renata, and his face twitched angrily, but then he suddenly said: "Come over here," and his wife slipped into the room and sat down with her strong, fat arms on the table.

"You did come alone?" she asked, looking anxiously at Renata. "Nobody saw you on the way?"

"Sure they did," Renata said. "Somebody saw me, a whole family, and I didn't come alone either but with a woman from my hotel. She is waiting for me on the road right now, and we plan to walk back together as well."

"What did I tell you!" the man said, and for a moment the woman looked terrified. Then she made a motion with both hands, as if they were two scales, one of which rose while the other sank. Not until much later did Renata know that at this moment the woman really had weighed something or drawn up a balance sheet, and on the one side of this balance sheet were the farm, the boats, and the cattle, life and freedom, and on the other side was the fate of a stranger. Renata saw only the woman's hand which dropped heavily on the table now and which the man seized and held down as if he wanted to prevent his wife from saying anything further. He leaned over and hung obliquely across the table. Renata wondered where she was, that's how still it was in the room, like at the bottom of a lake. But soon her hopes soared as the man proceeded to give her an address, a house she could go to twenty minutes away, not by following the road but by taking the narrow path along the lake. You could see the house from the garden all right, he said; the only thing was you had to go around the point. It was the parsonage, the owner was a farmer and a fisherman; he had two boats and went out on the lake at night.

"The house in the elder bushes?" Renata asked smiling, because now she would get to go there after all, to her real destination.

"Yes," the man said quickly, and now she must leave. His wife would just show her the way, and she needn't be afraid of the dog; it was chained. He suddenly seemed to be in a hurry to get rid of Renata. He almost pushed her out of the house with his hands and only whispered something to his wife at the door. Walking ahead of Renata like a lamb to the slaughter, all she said was: "Take a left, then a right, and then straight ahead," all this so softly that before Renata had turned the corner by the barn, she could hear a noise like the cranking of an old-fashioned telephone and the voice of the fisherman, but quite different sounding now, as if he were lowering it on purpose.

He is letting them know I'm on my way, she thought, but without any mistrust. Only the wife's behavior seemed strange to her, for now she opened a garden gate and pointed to a path in the bullrushes; then without even saying goodbye she turned around and disappeared. Renata called after her to thank her and quickly walked on. She was upset that she hadn't been able to get back on the road to let the district judge's wife know. Besides, the house in the elder bushes seemed much easier to get to if you took the road, for the path among the rushes, beautiful as it might be, didn't just wander around this one long point but around several other smaller ones as well, and again and again the house disappeared from Renata's view. Sometimes she could see nothing but the gray forests of reeds and the pale surface of the water, which the little black coots dashed across with bobbing heads. For a moment she thought the fisherman might have sent her in this direction in order to follow her—barefoot, silently, quickly—to take her money. She would not have been given a chance to turn him in, she was in his hands. She began to run, her heart beating violently. Almost with relief she now heard over there on the road the sound of an engine, a car, driving up full speed and coming to a screeching halt nearby. Then the elder bushes were there again, quite close now, above the crown of reeds. Renata slackened her pace. She thought about the house, considering with her lucid mind all the pros and cons of buying it. She already saw herself sitting on a balcony above the lake with her young sons. It wouldn't be hard to build a balcony like that. Then she could call a halt to all these rescue operations. This is where she wanted to stay and tend her garden till the war was over and the whole business done with. When the roof and the yellow housewall suddenly emerged in front of Renata, and when she saw an old man not very far away busying himself with a red net that was hanging there, she had to pull herself together first. Her mission wasn't accomplished yet. The little pixie had to be brought to safety first. She could already envision her sitting in the boat that night wrapped in the red fishing net, her delicate little old woman's hand poking out. As she thought about this, she suddenly smelled gasoline. It warned her, or could have warned her, if she hadn't been so intent on putting this last job behind her in the best way she knew and then have some peace. She took the bills out of her purse again and, holding them firmly between her fingers, approached the red net where the man was sitting with an old hat on his head, looking strangely still.

"Good evening," she said, giving her spiel, this time throwing caution to the winds. If he would agree to take a little Jewish girl across the lake tonight, she would make it worth his while.

She didn't get an answer, nor was it possible to get one. The house was empty, and the owners had been arrested. The man in the old hat was just a scarecrow leaning up against the red net. But from behind the net, two men in black uniforms appeared and grabbed Renata by the arms, the bills fell on the ground, the trap snapped shut.

At moments like this, you think of secondary things first. When the two men pushed Renata into the car, which had been hidden behind the house, and drove her into town, the first thing she thought about was the district judge's wife; then she thought about the little girl whose parents would be waiting in vain for the good news; and finally she thought about herself and about the high stakes she had been playing for, for her life, really, nothing less, nothing more. "How could you do a thing like that?" her uniformed companions said angrily. And now instead of these men, to the right and to the left of her in the back seat, were her own sons asking: "Mother, how could you?" Suddenly even she herself no longer understood what all she had ventured for a strange little girl, namely the future of her own sons. Don't be afraid, she whispered to them, smiling as she rode through the sweet, summery countryside in a cloud of dust—a modern heroine. The red of evening was warm, but the green northern sky was icy cold. Renata wrapped her black cardigan more tightly around herself. Then she tightened her belt, this long, soft woolen belt with which she knotted the noose that evening in the prison and in which her fresh, brave face already hung extinguished when the guard walked in.

The Piece of Straw

It was shortly before twelve o'clock when I found the letter. Honestly, I did find it, I didn't go hunting for it, didn't pull it out of the pocket by accident when I was brushing his suit. It poked out of a book, and the book was not on Felix's night stand but on the living room table with all the other newspapers for everyone to see. I didn't read the whole letter either, just the first couple of words: I miss you so much, darling. At first these words didn't mean anything to me at all, I just wanted to see the handwriting, an open hand with big beautiful downward loops and frequent spacing between the letters. That signifies fear of contact, I thought, and it was only then that I realized what it said. I found myself laughing although this certainly wasn't any laughing matter. Not until a few moments later did it occur to me that the letter could be for Felix. Once I realized this, I stopped reading. I just finished the page, all tender words; then I put the letter back and closed the book.

I went out in the kitchen figuring something must be going on. After all, you don't write stuff like that for no reason. I started to fix lunch—putting on my apron, pouring grease in the skillet, onion slicer, round glass container pounding and turning, you don't even have to touch the onions, and you don't cry. Not that anyone cries these days. Crying is no longer in fashion just as fainting isn't. It's not the way it was when our grandmothers were alive, for then there was always a maid on hand or a hefty cook to catch you and loosen your corset and say, don't take it so hard, that's the way men are, mine was no different, or simply: You poor thing! I didn't faint, nor did I cry; the grease made such a nice crackling sound, and I didn't really have any reason to cry. Well, I thought, get the meat out of the refrigerator, open the door, close the door, a funny noise when the refrigerator door closes, soft and whooshy and yet firm, an unpleasant noise, always so final as if for the last time. The last time, refrigerator, the last time we were having lunch together, how did things go today, did anyone call, all of it for the last time. Why actually? What happened? Nothing happened, a lot happened; I was shocked the way you get when you touch a bad socket, it's just that I didn't want it to be true. No, I didn't want it to be true. I put the meat in the skillet to brown, the cutlets, raw and red on the one side, then golden brown, raw and red on the other side, then nicely brown.

No, I'm not going to feel bad, I thought, putting the skillet away. I sat down at the table to peel the potatoes, but also to give the matter some thought, and when I had peeled the first potato, I got furious and thought to myself that it would be all right for me to do it, but not for Felix. It would be all right for me to turn men's heads, because that's all deception anyway, nothing but a stupid pastime. Just for a moment you notice the eyes of a stranger light up, you know someone finds you attractive. But men are different, with men that simply won't do ...

I peeled six potatoes, then I stopped because I was no longer hungry. I was going to have just one because no one must notice, Felix least of all. I had no intention of bringing up the business about the letter, because I already knew that words are something terrible, and not until you write something down is it really true. So I took off my apron and went into the bedroom to fix myself up and play the happy young wife. Later on I would figure out what to do. But just as I was walking across the room, the doorbell rang. At first I didn't want to open the door because I was suddenly afraid of anyone who might show up, of anyone at all. But then I did open up after all, and it was just a delivery from the pharmacy. I unpacked it and put the items away in the bathroom. She will have to learn all about that now, I thought, what kind of soap he likes, what kind of toothpaste. There's a trick to using the razor, and if you don't know about that, it doesn't work. She will also have to learn how to make the bed, better tuck in the quilts right, and the hot water bottle goes all the way down, but maybe he won't want that anymore. No, of course, he won't want anything the way it was here, no lavender soap, no hard toothbrush, everything different, everything new. Once more everything brand-new.

That's the way I talked to myself as I sat in the bathroom on the edge of the tub and looked into the mirror. Not that young anymore, a few wrinkles from laughing, from thinking, simply from living, from the time that has passed. Wrinkles are like road maps, all the roads we have taken together. But I didn't ponder whether the woman who wrote him the letter could be younger than I, and I actually never thought about who it might be; all that didn't matter. I washed my face and then actually went into the bedroom, and then I thought: He will have to leave me the apartment, that would be even better. After all, he can't put her in my bed, and in any case, the person who wants out is the one who has got to go. If I keep the apartment, I could rent out a room, maybe the front room, the couch would make a nice bed over there in the corner, it still has a pretty cover. The wardrobe from the landing would have to be moved, drawers would have to be made for underwear, and hangers would have to be bought. The lamp with the green shade, no, it won't do; I would have to get another shade. I'll have to get shelf paper, beautiful rose-colored paper with wavy lines or the kind with the little boats. I've been wanting to get some of that for quite a while.

Even I finally found these thoughts amusing, all the things you dream up, you know, and maybe the letter was quite old, and maybe that business was finished a long time ago. Perhaps it wasn't over yet, but it might pass. And then I thought about the advice they always give you for these eventualities in the syndicated columns in women's magazines, advice from someone who calls herself Aunt Anna or Aunt Emilie. Try setting a festive table, they say, or put on your prettiest dress, or get yourself a new hairdo, and how about a glass of wine, darling, I feel like celebrating tonight!

In the meantime the phone rang, but just once, as so often happens when someone realizes he has dialed the wrong number and quickly hangs up again. But it occurred to me it could so easily be Felix calling from the office. Why do I suddenly have tears in my eyes? Anyway, that doesn't matter; after all, he can't see me. He can only hear my voice, and my voice is very tender and loving. What did you say? You won't be home for lunch? Whether that makes any difference? Of course not. Not at all. In fact, it's just as well. I still have some ironing to do, and I was going to go and have my hair done anyway. No, I wasn't planning anything special for lunch. I haven't even started cooking yet. Is everything all right? Me? Great. Such a nice day. See you tonight, sure …

Yes, that's how I would play it! Make it very easy for him, be very carefree. And that's the way I would act when he got home as well.

Actually he should have been here by now. It was past one thirty, and he was always on time. Besides, he was always starved by noon, and he knew we were having cutlets today, which he loved. But maybe he didn't even care anymore. Maybe he was so late because he was still sitting with her in a bar drinking, and maybe he was looking at his watch right now and saying: It's past one thirty already, and she's waiting. I've got to run.

She is waiting, I thought. She, that's me. He figures he better not let me wait. He's afraid of me. But that's not the important thing. The important thing is the third person. I'm that third person. The third person, the bad person, the spoilsport, "she." I am the yellow flower with the one strange petal and the long red tongue, and now I'm supposed to trap him once more, little hors d'oeuvre, tuna with peas, sure, Aunt Emilie, thanks a lot for your good advice. That's not going to prevent him from suddenly putting down his knife and fork and saying: I'm truly sorry, but I don't love you anymore; I'm so sorry, but please let me go.

Of course, I would let him go. By all means, more power to you. I don't need you in my life, no one needs anyone else in his life; I don't even need the apartment, and I don't need any of your money. I can get my old job back; I could have got it back a long time ago, but you never wanted me to. There is something nice about working in an office: Good morning, Herr Schneider. Did we get any mail today? Good morning, Fräulein Lili. Is your tooth any better? Really, can't we get some heat in this place? As I was saying, about the boss's birthday party, ...

All these thoughts went through my head as I stood by the window looking out, through the curtains actually so that Felix wouldn't see me standing there. It was such a nice day in February, bright and dazzling. Every year you forget how strong the light can be even in February. Right now they are rolling the Catherine wheels down the mountains and throwing the ugly straw dolls down the wells. We once watched that together, Felix and I. We have experienced so many wonderful things together, and now I guess he doesn't want to remember any of them anymore. Now everything is to become null and void and be gray and dead, and that's the worst thing of all, that there won't be any future or any past. That ugly, yellow straw doll will go right down the well, now spring is coming, now everything will be completely new.

In the meantime I had to step aside a couple of times because some people I knew walked by: Herr Wehrle, the schoolteacher who lives next door, and Frau Seidenspinner who lives in number five. I could imagine the gossip: Did you hear the latest? Poor woman! It almost made me sick, because I can't stand pity. Pity is like hot broth with beads of fat on it; there is something terribly aggressive about it. Just what gives Frau Seidenspinner the right to feel sorry for me? In cases of death, all right, then the good Lord himself is in charge, then there's no problem. Then he could come home with tender words on his lips: You were all I had, and everything was wonderful. Then they can't say later on: She had been letting herself go lately, you really can't blame him.

Oh, the stupid things that went through my head. What do I care about the neighbors? It wouldn't occur to me to run over to them and complain the way Herta once did, saying: After all these years of marriage ... and I've always been a good wife to him, can you imagine? For of course I wasn't a good wife to Felix. If I were, he wouldn't want to leave me and have someone write love letters to him and maybe even write love letters himself, and he wouldn't be afraid to come home and think: How am I going to tell her?

All this time I stood looking out the window, and suddenly a man came around the corner who had Felix's bearing and Felix's gait and who wore a dark blue winter coat. My heart skipped a beat the way it does when a plane suddenly loses altitude. I tried to look natural but soon felt that I couldn't. The man came closer, only it wasn't Felix at all but a stranger, and I asked myself just what kinds of games we were playing. I

25

could actually leave right away, even before he came home. I could go into town and sit down in a café, in the dreary, dusty one near the stock exchange, the one with all the mirrors, where my image would be reproduced a hundred times over, a hundred times the same lonely woman. I could leaf through the magazines there and smoke and stare into space. You could kill a few hours that way. A couple of hours later I could go to a movie, one show and then another, and then it would suddenly be night. Then it really was night, and Felix would have to call the police, which would be most embarrassing for him. Your wife is missing, you say? What? What she was wearing? I have no idea.

It was two o'clock right now, and I couldn't stand there any longer. I sat down on a chair and turned on the radio. As always when you want to listen to something edifying or uplifting, I was obliged to listen to the flood stages, all the rivers in the country, take your pick. The Weser was the worst, and the Weser is quite far away. And then the phone rang again, but this time not just once. I was certain that this time it would be Felix, and sure enough, that's who it was. I still remembered exactly what it was I wanted to tell him, the way I had tried it out earlier, tender, loving voice, but just then I wasn't up to it because of the dreary café and the rivers and the police, and things came out altogether differently, something like this:

Oh, it's you. (Wrong, wrong!)

What was that? You won't be home for lunch? (I can't seem to hit the right tone of voice!)

Sure, that's fine; after all, it's such a nice day.

It wouldn't be worth your while? No, of course not.

I sound funny? What do you mean funny?

No, nothing is wrong. At least, nothing that would interest you.

Why not?

I should think you'd know that better than I. And so on. All of it in this dreadful, offended tone of voice, which I didn't want to use, but that's the way it came out, the straw doll, so pressed and squashed, so awful, and finally I just kept talking so that he would hang up, so that there would be an end to it, an end to everything. And since he didn't hang up, I simply didn't say anything, nothing at all, as I sat there with the receiver pressed to my ear. Are you still there? he asked very sweetly, completely bewildered, and then he finally hung up. I hung up, too, and stood there hating myself and hating him as well, because it was his fault that I had behaved like that, the third person, the heavy, the straw doll thrown down the well, goodbye. And then I thought no, I might as well finish the letter since that's the kind of person I was, the kind of person they imagined me to be, and apparently that's how I'd always been, as long as I had lived, the whole time.

I went into the living room, got the letter out of the book, and lit a cigarette, which I should have done a long time ago. Why do I always think at two different levels? At the upper level it says there are no happy marriages, and at the lower level it says oh, please come back. I start to read the letter once again, skimming the first page. I already know what it says. On the second page there is very little, and on the third and fourth nothing at all. On the second page it says: "Has it been only five days, actually just four and a half? Don't forget to stop by the laundry; our things must have been ready for quite a while. Bye for now, dearest Franz. I love you, take care. Maria."

"Bye for now, dearest Franz, take care; bye for now, dearest Franz, take care." I must have repeated this ten times, and then I started to laugh like a madwoman, because this letter wasn't for Felix at all but for a man by the name of Franz Kopf. His name was also in the book, and the book was a business text, and except for the fact that he had borrowed this book from a fellow who was a bit sloppy, Felix had nothing at all to do with it. I told myself that, but it had really gotten to me. I guess I should have jumped and laughed and sung, but I simply couldn't. I sat there and stared, and I felt as if I had fallen into a deep well and was now in the process of climbing back up, but strange to say, I couldn't get all the way up, and it didn't get quite bright again.

I tried to climb out of that dark well all afternoon, and by evening I was finally out. When Felix came home, I laughed and said: I'm sorry I was so grouchy when we talked on the phone. I had a terrible headache, but thank God it's gone. I take it you feel better now, said Felix, you look good. But then he suddenly asked: What's that? and reached over to pull something out of my hair: a long, pale piece of straw. And just where did that come from, pray, tell?

The Old Manor House

A few years ago in an Alsatian court a case was tried that aroused widespread sympathy. A man was accused of arson, and the judge had imposed a fairly severe sentence. The man, who was still young—thirty years old at the most—refused legal counsel and made a long speech in his own defense. In so doing, he made no attempt to deny his guilt or to shift the blame to others. He was fully aware that he deserved punishment for his action, but when he explained his side, his guilt seemed to become something completely different, something much more universal. Thus he was not acquitted in the end, but the reflective mood that his speech evoked in everyone in the courtroom had a favorable effect on the determination of the degree of punishment. People realized that the motive for the arson, which destroyed an old manor house, was not a desire for wealth or some kind of insurance fraud, and it was certainly not selfishness. On the contrary, an uncontrollable madness had motivated the accused to commit this destructive deed. It seemed reasonable to consider such madness a pathological condition, and the case would surely have been tried along those lines if the accused had not opposed this most vehemently from the very beginning. All clarifications and at the same time confusing issues followed from the story of the man, who at the request of the high court got up immediately and held forth for half an hour without any written notes. All the while he regarded the court officials, the jurors, or the public with a candid expression while at the same time looking at no one in particular with an almost imbecile, tense face. The only favor he requested was a slate, on which he proceeded to sketch something, a kind of map with wavy lines, stripes, squares, and circles, to which he kept pointing throughout his explanation. As he sketched and erased and pointed, it occurred to some of the jurors and guests of the court that his hands were noticeably strong and sunburnt, the hands of someone who, if not a farmhand, had nevertheless done farm work for quite some time. The composed and elevated manner in which the accused expressed himself did not seem to square with his physique. As a result the members of the audience were not sure whom they were dealing with and at first followed the explanations of the accused with a certain skepticism, even with whispered comments. But the man did not find this disconcerting. He had hardly finished his simple sketch before both the jurors and the judges had the strange and somewhat humiliating impression that the accused had not actually delivered his testimony before them but rather before a person who was not present at all and who possibly could not be mentioned in the same breath with all the people who were gathered there.

"This is the manor house by the name of Trois Sapins," the accused began, pointing to a little square he had drawn on the slate. "It belongs, or belonged until a short time ago, to Baron d'Agoult, and the vineyards and fields I have sketched here also belonged to him. He sold his little property a few months ago so that, as you have heard, the plaintiff is not he but the buyer, a real estate developer."

As the accused said this, the general interest turned to some gentlemen who had served as witnesses earlier and who apparently represented the developer. The above-mentioned baron had apparently been invited to the proceedings but had not appeared. After having used his name just once, the accused referred to him as "Monsieur," and every time the subject turned to him, his face became strangely sad and wistful. "I must say something about this village and this house," he continued. "I must remind you that there are places that your heart yearns for even if you're not born there and even if you have no real reason to be there. You experience a strong and passionate love for a place like that, and you find out you're not the only one. You try to figure out what the reason is for this exaggerated, indeed, almost unhealthy inclination, and I have often tried to find an explanation for my own attraction to Trois Sapins. For a while I thought I was just in love with the countryside, which changes so strangely there, like the wind blows, suddenly lovely and mild, then wild and mysterious, one moment seemingly part of the gentle stream beds and the next of the rough mountain forests with their loneliness and their wolf packs. Then again I thought the real attraction was the house itself, a rather dilapidated place, with its strange smell of old stairs, its paintings of the ancestors and its worn silk-covered furniture, and outside its three fir trees, the crown and glory of an old Calvary mountain. But finally I came to the conclusion that there is no accounting for things like that."

With these words the accused turned to his slate again. "This," he said pointing with his finger to a long rectangle, "is the barn where the horse belonging to Monsieur's father was stabled. When I came to Trois Sapins, this horse was already dead. It was very old when Monsieur's father rode it through the forests at the foot of the Ballon d'Alsace, but on the scattered farms up there, there were still some old-timers left who remembered the lonely rider."

At this moment the judge gestured impatiently. "Let's get on with the story," he said sternly. But the accused remained unperturbed.

"Monsieur's parents," he said, "were part of Sach. When I came to Trois Sapins, they were not dead in the real sense of the word, although

29

they had been resting in the cemetery for the longest time. They were alive and a great burden to Monsieur, just like everything else was a great burden to him—his house, his property, and his employees. For he could do nothing right for anyone, Monsieur couldn't, not for the living and not for the dead. Everyone found fault with him, and not until it was all over, did they possibly notice that he, too, had been somebody and that they had loved him."

"What do you mean 'when it was all over'?" the judge asked.

"When Monsieur finally had enough," the accused answered. "At that point I was no longer at Trois Sapins," he continued. "But I heard he had sold the house and the estate, and it was like being stabbed in the heart. I remembered the day I first arrived at Trois Sapins. I was right out of the army, and I asked Monsieur for food and work, work that had nothing to do with my profession, like hauling earth, digging up potatoes, picking apples and putting them away for the winter, building pig pens. If you have grown up on a farm, you know what all that entails and that the work never ends, not all year long. Monsieur knew that I had studied at a university and wanted to become a teacher, and sometimes he thought all this really wasn't for me and I was wasting my time. But then I explained to him why this type of work seemed to make more sense than anything else at the moment; and because I was handy and he could use me, he didn't say anything more about it. Besides, he liked me and asked me a couple of times to have dinner with him and be part of the family. But I would have had to change clothes and eat properly and converse properly, and I had forgotten about all that sort of thing in the military and wanted nothing to do with it anymore. So I ate in the kitchen like the other farmhands, and in the evening I would sit in my room, listen to the radio, and gaze at the three fir trees and the valley. Sometimes I thought about Monsieur and about what might be going on in his head when he walked across his fields and meadows with a worried look on his face, and once I wondered if perhaps Monsieur, who owned everything here, might be the only one who longed to be elsewhere, God only knows where, in a foreign country or at sea. But then again I thought maybe he simply had problems. After all, after the war it wasn't as easy to make a go of it here as it was over there in Germany, for example, where every farmhouse was spruced up and added on to, and where many new farm machines colored red and shiny blue were already moving about in the fields. And while I was off duty and sat contemplating the summer evening, Monsieur was sitting at his desk over his accounts …

"Maybe you're wondering why Monsieur, who after all was single and alone, was calculating so hard and worrying about things. But actually he was not alone. He had three sisters, all of whom were very pretty and all of whom were married and living in Paris: Madame Berthe, Madame Flore, and Madame Julie, whom everyone called Chérie. Of these sisters now one, then another would come for a visit, and as soon as they arrived, they would kick off their heels and step out of their finery, get their jackets out of the closet, and run through the forest and across the meadows, their long hair flowing in the wind. Because their hair was reddish and their movements violent, they always reminded me of hurricanes, which you can never quite figure out and never hold on to. They also had a strange penchant for sitting in their old, worn-out children's chairs and for sleeping in their narrow children's beds, and I think they actually didn't want to grow up at all but would just as soon be children at home forever. Indeed, they behaved like children, demanding money from Monsieur, the way children demand money for candy from their parents, without having any idea what money is and where it comes from. Monsieur paid for their permanents and for their medical bills, and he was happy when they came to visit all right, but it annoyed him that they meddled in his affairs and always made a fuss whenever they noticed any kind of change. Why was the yellow hedge rose withering, they cried angrily, and what happened to the goldfish, and who put those ugly chicken coops in the meadow? Every time I felt very sorry for Monsieur because it was finally asking too much that he always just play this father role and nothing else. I tried to make that clear to the ladies, especially Madame Chérie, whom I liked the best although she was the most childish of all. But Madame Chérie didn't understand at all. 'Just like Dad,' she said angrily, 'then he could be happy;' and then she started to tell about her father, all the old stories that I already knew by heart ..."

At this point the accused paused and smiled to himself, and it seemed as if he had completely forgotten where he was going. But he pulled himself together and explained that the young ladies had had great confidence in him. "As soon as one of them arrived," he said, "I was interrupted in my work and asked to come along to this place or the other and give my opinion. They called me by my first name and often commented on how nice it was that I was there and that I mustn't ever leave. But finally I did plan to leave. I had a chance to get a scholarship and wanted to continue my studies, but I kept postponing it from month to month. I also refrained from mentioning it so that I wouldn't be forced to go through with my decision.

That was last summer which was so warm and lovely. The haying went very nicely, but there wasn't a lot of hay because it had been so dry early on, and the grass hadn't had a chance to grow. Madame Chérie visited in July; she would busy herself in the flower garden pulling weeds, which nobody else had time for, and Monsieur would go down to the garden and keep her company. I remember very well the afternoon I saw the two standing down there talking. I was just walking past the house when I heard the phone ringing, and because nobody moved, I ran up the steps to the hall and answered it. It was a gentleman from the bank wanting to talk to Monsieur, and I went down to the garden to tell him, and then I stayed a moment with Madame Chérie, who was crouching again while pulling the shallow-rooted, swaying weeds out of the soil. 'Do stay and keep me company,' said Madame Chérie, and then she suddenly thrust her head back and said, 'It's too nice here; and the fact that everything must end just about spoils one's enjoyment.'

I wondered why Madame Chérie would say that sort of thing and why her eyes filled with tears as she said it, because Madame Chérie was very happily married and had two lovely little children and a beautiful home in Paris. It also occurred to me that Monsieur's sisters hardly ever brought their husbands and children along to Trois Sapins and how strange and unnatural that was. Madame Chérie buried her tear-stained face in the flowering phlox, and when Monsieur came back, she laughed again and tossed back her long curly hair. But I noticed that she took a quick and careful look at her brother's face; as a matter of fact, so did I, and I found it changed and dead serious. Surely Madame Chérie would now ask Monsieur who had called and why, but she waited a moment, and just then the phone in the house started to ring again. Because the three of us were very still just then, we heard it quite distinctly, and this time Monsieur did not wait to see if anyone else would answer it but turned on his heels and hurried through the garden and up the steps. He didn't return for the longest time, and when he finally did come out of the house, he just called to his sister and said not to expect him home for dinner, for he had to go into town.

Not until much later did I figure out what those calls were all about and that the moment Monsieur went over to the garage, the fate of Trois Sapins was sealed. At that time, that is, on that evening and in the following days and weeks, you couldn't tell what Monsieur felt. He knew how to pull himself together when he had to, but I thought he seemed more concerned about his sister than normally. He would frequently go for walks with her in the forest and make different little excursions with her in the area, which he had never done before because gasoline was so expensive. Madame Chérie did not learn anything from him, however, and when I took her to the station at the end of August, she said it would not be long before she would be coming back, at Christmas time at the latest she would be back. And then she added that it had been especially beautiful this time, more beautiful than for a long time; in fact, not since her childhood had it been like that. I helped get her suitcase on the train and stood outside and waved, and then I drove home and told Monsieur that I wanted to go back to school in Strasbourg starting in the winter semester. Monsieur looked at me almost frightened for a moment, but then he said it was not his place to try to hold me back, and suddenly he looked quite relieved.

In the fall I really did leave. I felt very bad that day, and even for many days prior to that, and when I said goodbye to Monsieur, I asked if I could come out for Christmas. I asked him that just at the last minute, because I thought it might have occurred to Monsieur himself to invite me. Monsieur didn't look at me but said quickly, 'Of course, that goes without saying,' but just like someone who didn't at all believe there would be a Christmas or like someone whose mind was elsewhere. Nevertheless, I was glad I asked, and in the first few weeks in town I often pictured how it would be at Christmas. I remembered the four or five Christmas Eves I had spent in Trois Sapins. Every time the föhn had played like a mighty organ at the edge of the forest, and every time it had been in the fifties and quite warm, and violets were in bloom.

But then one day I saw in the paper a picture of Trois Sapins. I was angry right away because it was a poor gray picture that didn't at all reflect any of the silken glow of the sky, the unusual growth of the old fir trees, and the beauty with which the double outside staircase rises toward the front door. I read what it said below the picture, and I had to read it a couple of times, because at first I didn't understand at all. The article was about a builder who had bought a number of lots here and there in the countryside including Trois Sapins, where he was thinking of putting up a bunch of cheap houses. According to the account, the company had also taken over the old manor house from the owner of the estates belonging to Trois Sapins; there was supposed to be a tourist lodge and a restaurant.

At that point I put my newspaper down and excused myself from the dinner table, and that was the moment I mentioned earlier, the moment when I was reminded of all the things that had happened, the most incredible things, and there is nothing I would have liked more than to drop everything and get on the train right away. But I didn't get away until a week later, on December 20, and in the meantime I'd had a chance to think about a lot of things, including the fact that the whole thing might be a mistake and that you frequently read the craziest stories in the paper. On the way from the station to Trois Sapins, which takes about three quarters of an hour and on which you pass quite a few houses, I made sure not to get into conversation with anyone. I just waved and laughed and kept walking, acting as if I had never been away and was just out for a stroll. It was already late afternoon, the mild, gentle storm played the pipes of the organ at the edge of the forest, it was quickly getting dark. In

33

the old manor house, which you could see from fairly far away, there were no lights on, nor was there any light in the stables, and I figured right away that the newspaper must be right after all. There really wasn't anyone there anymore. The cattle and the horses were no longer in their stables, and no one was cooking in the kitchen. It was like a terrible nightmare to see the house on the hill almost sailing along like the ship of the flying Dutchman with nothing but dead people on board.

With all this, I couldn't help notice that something had already changed in the rambling village, that foundations had been dug and streets staked out. I also thought I could see an enormous structure in the dark like a new factory on which some lanterns were swinging high above like intoxicated stars, and although it was late, I thought I could hear the noise of cement mixers. The people I met had excited, hopeful looks on their faces as if a new and better age were dawning, and for a moment I felt ashamed and thought that people who didn't believe in the future were really committing a sin. But of course, that is not the way it was. It was just that in that house everything was supposed to remain the way it had always been. I wanted that not for myself but for Madame Berthe and Madame Flore and Madame Chérie, who otherwise would never run across the windy meadows again in their old jackets and who would never forgive their brother. For surely no one would ever be able to make clear to them what I had figured out for myself on this evening walk, namely that the bank had given Monsieur notice on the very day Madame Chérie was weeding the flower garden and that shortly thereafter the builder had called and made him the offer, which he had agreed to in his distress (or had in mind all along). They would realize after all this that they could no longer visit Trois Sapins, and in a cruel way they would suddenly be forced to grow up."

Having said this, the accused, whom no one had interrupted the entire time, again turned to his slate and his sketch. He traced a chalk line with his finger and showed where he had gone around the barn and where he had seen a pile of straw and some wood shavings apparently left behind by the movers. "It was at that moment," he said, "that I thought of setting fire to the old house at Trois Sapins and to prepare an end for it that truly was an end. In any case, I kept walking because I noticed a car sitting in the middle of the courtyard and because I knew right away it belonged to Monsieur. And then I saw Monsieur walking toward a ladder, which he had leaned against the house, with a crowbar in his hand, and I realized he was about to remove the little stone crest that was placed above the door. The door to the house stood wide open, and all the windows were open as well and rattled in the wind. It made such a noise that Monsieur didn't hear my steps, and not until I was close behind him and said good evening, did he turn around and look at me frightened.

'Let me do that,' I said, as I had said hundreds of times before when Monsieur started to do something he wasn't fit to do and which would have cost him too much time and energy. Monsieur might also be thinking about that just then, for he gave me the crowbar and smiled. I saw he looked pale but young, and I wondered what he would do now, and whether he considered this the fulfillment of an old dream. I didn't ask, however, but merely suggested that he leave, which he apparently intended to do anyway, for he had left his parking lights on, the motor was idling, and the luggage was stowed away. 'Yes,' he said, 'I'd be grateful to you if you would,' and then he quickly sat down behind the steering wheel as if he were running away. He didn't seem to find it strange at all that I was there, and I didn't find it strange that I had run into him. I only saw that he couldn't stand it there any longer, not one second longer. He shook my hand and pulled the car door shut, and when the car turned around in the courtyard, the beams from the headlights illuminated the rose beds one last time, then the double curved stone staircase, the unusual fir trees, the round basin of the fountain, before disappearing out the gate. I wandered around for a while longer, as long as it takes the driver to go down the hill and then around it and to have the hill and the house behind him and not see anything anymore. Then I put the crowbar away and got out the straw and the wood shavings and went over to the garage, which was empty except for a canister of gasoline that was still sitting there half full. I moved very calmly and very slowly as if in a trance. I hardly thought of anything at all except the fact that Madame Chérie surely never would understand why I set fire to the old house or for whom I did it, since all that was no concern of mine, and maybe a woman wouldn't understand that sort of thing anyway. But to me it seemed very right, that is, in a mysterious sort of way, that the wood shavings to which I held my lighter caught fire right away and that the storm then very quickly carried the flames through the empty rooms, soon filling the whole building. And even as the people screamed and came running from all directions, and the village fire fighters raced up the hill, I was still convinced that everything would be better if Trois Sapins would disappear completely from the face of the earth. That way it would go on forever, the way it always had been."

The Black Lake

A few days ago I read in the paper that Lake Albano had turned red this summer, blood red. According to the article the phenomenon was easily explained through the large-scale invasion of a certain variety of algae, the so-called blood algae, which produces a red dye while in bloom. Needless to say, I didn't give much consideration to this scientific explanation. I pictured the lake, this deep-set black eye within its frame of tree-covered slopes with its bright and cheerful villages on the hilltops and the somber melancholy of the crater opening. It seemed easy enough to understand that the water had turned the color of blood simply because it was a mysterious, even cursed body of water and had been so since time immemorial. Not even the Pope himself could alter the situation, although he lived on top of the mountain in the summertime, not toward the lake to be sure but on the other side, from where you could see the vineyards, the fertile fields on which the long-horned white cattle and the bright-colored tractors pulled the plow—and far out there the bright strip of the sea. Could this be the Devil grinning behind the Holy Father's back? Yes, that's surely what they thought about the lake, at least in the early days when people were more attuned to the demons of a place, when they didn't give nature a gentle kick in the side like an old circus horse making its rounds, while you stand on top of it and jump and have your fun, as they do these days. Most likely the inhabitants living along the lakeshore wouldn't have lost this sensitivity if the tourists hadn't arrived and taught them otherwise.

Yes, surely it was the tourists' fault that the lake had lost its mysterious look over the last few years. When they went for walks up above in the allee of oaks around Castel Gandolfo, they didn't talk about food and prices and love, as one might expect. They would explain to their wives and children the battles that had been fought between Rome and Alba-longa, and then they would shrug disparagingly and say: "Can you believe it? What a beautiful lake … If it were just fifteen kilometers from our town, what you wouldn't find in the way of weekend cottages and bath-houses with red and blue-painted gangways, cafés with terraces overlooking the lake, and restaurants with dance floors and colorful lanterns at night." And as they said this, they looked down at the water surface deep below, which didn't have one single boat on it, and at the steep slopes whose dusty green was unmarred by one single white villa. And when a cloud happened to cover the sun and an icy wind rose from the deep, they probably made a couple of derogatory remarks about being "taken for a ride" here in the sunny south. But they felt nothing of the demonic nature of the place.

The locals, too, didn't notice it for a while. Money found its way into the area, and highways were built. Where these blue asphalt roads cut through the vineyards and the oak and chestnut forests, there was no more solitude left. The city folks who invaded the places on the hilltop in droves every Sunday soon began driving down to the lake and taking a good look around. A young local fellow rented a little cabin from which he dispensed drinks, and during the next year he added to this venture a modest boat rental. Needless to say, people who rowed out on the lake on these hot summer days also wanted to go swimming, and so a row of cabanas went up. Because speed alone, not to mention the merry clatter of motors, gives people a sense of being alive, other vehicles had to be added, some kind of aquatic car, fire red and bright blue, in which lovers sat clinging to each other as they raced around the black lake. Since the wooden deck with its wrought-iron chairs soon wasn't good enough for guests who were used to better things, Antonio, a newly-wed waiter from Rome, ventured with his father-in-law's money to build on to the only house that was located at the long side of the lake and at a considerable distance from the village of Marino and to open a restaurant there. The fact that the road along the lake was rocky and often flooded, in fact, almost impassable, only added to the charm for the car-happy excursionists, whom the young innkeeper provided with little rest areas between flowering oleander and with tables and chairs under shady trees, and to whom he cheerfully served his delicious meals. Most likely some of the wealthier people, who soon dined at his place in ever greater numbers, planned to build summer homes nearby and spoke of dropping in on the mayor on the way home. Bathing suits were brought along. The young people jumped into the water from the little footbridge in front of the restaurant. A table, which the owner had placed there to warn people about the dangerous currents in the lake, was taken apart one day by a couple of boys who needed it for a float.

Thus this last visible reminder of the mystery of the place disappeared. At least, it seemed harmless now, as if controlled and subdued by the friendly whitewashed house, a paradise for lovers, who strolled down the narrow lake path after dinner, where they could hide from people's curious glances between oaks and chestnut trees. Antonio, the young owner, was the soul of this booming venture. His wife Rita was at his side, friendly and lively, and their little son was already running around with plates and silverware as well as showing the approaching cars where to park. Although he had never been a churchgoer, Antonio was often happy now that he had named his son Eugenio, which was also the name of the esteemed summer guest at Castel Gandolfo, of whom he thought gratefully and as a good neighbor and patron saint of his son.

One evening when the sky shone golden above the village of Castel Gandolfo and the trees up there on the hilltop were silhouetted against the sky, he called his son and pointed to a tree, the shape of which looked like a person in blessing gesture. Little Eugenio, who had just stepped into the garden from the lake path, obliged and came over next to him. He looked up, but then with icy fingers he took his father's hand and said that now he, too, wanted to show his father something. Without saying anything on the way or answering any of his father's questions, Eugenio dragged him down to the place he had come from. When his mother leaned out the window, her face flushed from working over a hot stove, and called after the two in her resonant young voice, the boy just shook his head angrily, pushed open the garden gate, and dragged his father down the narrow path through the oak shrubbery. There was the lake to the right, whereas the hill rose to the left. The sun had disappeared now, and with an excited murmur the little waves washed the tree roots on the shore. There was nothing here like a sandy beach. Around a bend, two older children emerged, playmates of little Eugenio's, strong, unruly fellows with whom the owner proceeded to joke. They didn't respond or jump up but stayed strangely stiff and almost paralyzed where they were, on the slope that is, twenty or thirty meters above the path along the shore next to a great big tree stump with something white poking out of it. When the owner saw the boys' greenish faces and felt his son's hand trembling in his own, he realized the children must have found something that frightened them. He ordered little Eugenio to stay put and quickly walked up to the tree stump, in which there really was something shocking: an unclothed body, a body without a head, that had been brutally forced into the wood.

I'm not going to tell you all about this murder, which was never completely solved. Although the newspapers at the time were full of all the speculations, investigations, false leads and correct ones, clues leading nowhere for weeks on end, I don't exactly remember the details. I only know that no one ever suspected the restaurant owner on the lake. He was called as a witness but never charged with anything, although the crime had been committed close to his house. The clinical, almost professional way in which the head, now lost and maybe lying at the bottom of the lake, had been severed from the torso, seemed to indicate that a butcher might have committed the murder. It was a masterpiece of carving, and at first they suspected mainly the butchers and meat cutters. The poor remaining body was that of a young woman, who was at an early stage of pregnancy. After a careful check of all the girls who had since left town, they assumed she was a domestic servant from Sicily, and her family was summoned from the island for identification of the body. However, what the head—hair and eyes, cheeks, temples and mouth—tells us about a human being (I mean that only these features can actually identify it) apparently became clear when the poor peasants looked at the hands and feet and were suddenly supposed to confirm what they didn't want to be true in the first place: yes, that was their child. This dark, silent, and not exactly pretty girl had apparently used her day off to make an excursion with an admirer, a boat trip on the lake. She had said nothing to her employer about this. They also couldn't attribute any previous love affairs to her; in fact, she didn't even seem to have any male friends. Whether or not the couple had stopped at Antonio's place before the horrible end to their excursion could not be determined since both the head and the clothes were missing. The boat keeper had rented boats out to a number of young couples that afternoon, and they had all been returned. It was not possible to ascertain whether one person had gone out in the company of another but come back alone. After all, the second person could have gotten off anywhere, for example at Antonio's pretty restaurant. There was talk for a while about a soldier, also about a sailor, but the investigations in the barracks and on the ships didn't turn up anything. In short, after many wasted efforts on the part of the police, things gradually quieted down around the dead woman and even more so along the lake shore and in Antonio's restaurant, which had been frequented by criminal investigators and numerous reporters, as well as by a number of curiosity seekers for several weeks. People did go out on the lake on occasion to speculate and to experience the horror of it all. But who could dream peacefully among the oleanders anymore or whisper sweet nothings? Who would be hungry for roast chicken in such close proximity to the curse-laden tree stump? And who would feel like going swimming in a lake where the head of the body could suddenly turn up, now surely disgustingly decayed and nibbled at by fishes?

Such disinclination didn't become obvious until the following spring. In late fall, when the days grew short and the winds became icy, Antonio closed up his restaurant as he had in the past and left with his wife and son for the suburbs of Rome to stay with his parents-in-law, with whom he enjoyed a good relationship. He found work in the city through the winter, and in the restaurants where he worked, people would occasionally point to him and whisper: That's the owner of the restaurant on the lake, or that's the fellow who knows everything about the woman with the head chopped off. They probably also tried to find out what he knew once in a while, though not very often and less frequently so as the winter wore on, since new and equally inexplicable atrocities already had taken hold of their imagination by then. It was a big relief for Antonio, who loved his wife and son more than anything in the world, that little Eugenio played as he normally did and that Rita, to, soon seemed to have forgotten the gruesome incident. He began to look forward to spring and to the reopening of his restaurant even before Easter. He went out there already in April to check out everything and to fix things up. His wife and son soon followed, and the parents-in-law, too, spent a Sunday out there. Antonio and his father-in-law, who had invested large sums of his savings in the venture, now walked through the premises, considering expansion and improvements, especially an extension of the upper story, by means of which they could gain space for guest rooms. In the past, a lot of the guests had expressed a desire to stay overnight, even for a longer period of time. Surely one could count on a good income in the hot months. Soon they started to saw, hammer, and pound. Boards and glass panes were brought in, and Antonio, who threw himself into these jobs, felt the last traces of stress vanish. When the extension was finished and the glaziers were painting their strange serpentine symbols on the freshly puttied windows, the most beautiful time of year had arrived: May with its even warmth and its wildflowers, and on the weekends the roads through the campagna began to fill with long columns of cars as with migrations of ants or beetles. Antonio had stocked his kitchen and his cellar, local girls had been commended to Rita's supervision, and early in the morning little Eugenio was all ready to show the approaching cars where to park in the enlarged and newly paved parking lot. But the lot remained unused, not just this early morning but all day long as well, and the white-covered tables stood empty.

The fact that a visit to the restaurant left much, in fact, everything to be desired on this first beautiful Sunday could, after all, be explained in many different ways: the evenings were still cool, the dazzling sun of the Latin beach was still appreciated more than the cool shade of the forest and the mountains. But then the weather changed again. It turned humid and hot as in mid-summer, and little Eugenio still stood in vain in the parking lot with the little flag his mother had sewn. The tables in the garden were still empty and the newly constructed rooms unused.

In August I was out there once. I played with little Eugenio before dinner, and while I was eating I chatted with his mother, this pretty, full-figured woman who wouldn't dream of losing courage. "The woman with the severed head is to blame for everything," she said, and little Eugenio, who was building a house of cards at the next table, sang "la de-ca-pi-ta-ta" as if it were a happy children's song and knocked over his house of cards. "But that won't last long," Rita continued. "By next year everybody will have forgotten."

As if her faith in the place were rewarded, a big foreign car silently drove up in front of the house. "What a lovely place," the tourists exclaimed, and then they had the deck chairs brought out, and they put on their bathing suits. It was almost as if there had never been any problem here. But, of course, Antonio had not had a chance to stock up the way he used to. The chickens, which were butchered on the spot, were scrawny, and when the guests left, I heard them making snide remarks about the food. The only other visitors that day were motorcyclists. The first one was a soldier with his girlfriend, lovers holding hands and casting shy glances into the dark bushes, behind which the narrow path ran along the lake. The second one was in uniform, too, but he didn't sit down or have anything to eat; instead he went straight into the house, and when I paid for my meal, I learned he had served Antonio a summons, a summons to court.

Needless to say, this summons was still in regard to the crime. But surely it was just a matter of detail, a confirmation that had been overlooked or something, I told myself as I slowly walked around the lake to Marino, but I couldn't get around the fact that the lake seemed terribly desolate and melancholy that evening. This melancholy seemed to rise from the water itself as from an immeasurable depth, but not so high that the fresh mountain breezes could seize hold of it and destroy it. Dark shadows covered the edge of the steep bank while the water, stirred by strange whirlpools, colored itself in the image of the evening sun. As in past years there was not a boat on the lake, and only from far away could happy voices and mandolin music be heard coming from the white terraces on the hilltop as if from a different, happier world. I went up there that day to meet some friends and as a result forgot all about the innkeeper Antonio and his family. Soon thereafter I returned to my own country and didn't get back to Rome until winter. But within the first few days, in one of the restaurants where Antonio used to help out during the winter months, I learned that the little family had not come back to town at all this time but had remained out there on the lake all by themselves.

When I say "all by themselves," no one here is likely to understand what I mean. After all, there were three of them and they had each other, and there might even have been an old housekeeper who went around closing the shutters in the evening. But for southern Europeans, this is a bitter loneliness. Because really to live they need grandparents and parents, aunts and uncles, brothers and sisters and their children. They need the piazza with its men's talk and the bar with its wheel of fortune and its arguments about politics. Noise is part of it, the noise of engines and human voices and human faces in passion and joy and pain. All this Antonio and Rita had to do without, and then, of course, there was the winter, which was unusually severe and seemed never to end this year. There were several heavy snowfalls, and the snow stayed on the ground for a long time, crusted and dirty. On the few sunny days icy winds would blow, and in between there would be one big black thaw after another. Dense layers of fog settled over the interior waterways and refused to lift, especially at the foot of the mountain. The paths along the lakeshore, wrecked by ice and washed out by mud from the mountain brooks, were impassable. Antonio's house, too, was cut off from the outside this way, and the innkeeper crossed the lake in his boat only for the most necessary shopping, appearing in the stores only briefly and looking deathly pale, like someone from another world. The people in Marino asked if he were ill, but he wasn't; none of them out there was, and in spite of the nasty weather they didn't go back to town nor did they write any letters of complaint to their friends and relatives in Rome. Antonio and Rita kept busy with all kinds of home improvements, with the firewood and the animals, and in the evenings they taught their little son to read and to write. One time the father picked up watercolors for the boy, and Eugenio used these to make a number of strange smears and smudges the subject of which was a kind of water nymph, only one without a body whose neck turned right into a scaly fish tail. Antonio noticed these drawings but didn't make a fuss, just as he displayed a nice and even temper when dealing with his son and his wife during these weeks. One evening, however, he went out the door one more time, as he was wont to do, and this time he took his gun with him and angrily told his son, who wanted to come along, to get back in the house. That was at the time of the last thaw, a stormy night, the fire crackling in the fireplace, the lake gurgling and hissing, and the tree branches rattling like sabers against each other. So it happened that Antonio's wife didn't hear the shot that was fired out there and that only much later, when she ran out to look for Antonio and called his name, she stumbled in the dark and fell. And what she had stumbled over was her husband's body, what she gripped and embraced were his cold limbs, and what moistened her lips was his blood.

They later attributed Antonio's suicide to the weather and to his loneliness. They also said that his father-in-law had refused to lend him any more money and had asked to have the old loan repaid and that the two men got into an argument about it. Besides, they also said (not the court but all the people in the area) that Antonio had become a suspect in the case after all, and the more time went by without the real criminal being found, the more the innkeeper took the gossip to heart. And then, of

42

course, there were people who thought Antonio really was the murderer, and now, plagued by a bad conscience, he had atoned for his sin.

Needless to say, I don't believe a word of it. I'm more inclined to think there are still places on our technically oriented earth and in the middle of the noisy dwellings where people live that belong to the spirits. I think these spirits, misunderstood and neglected, crave first one victim and then another, and only then is everything all right. Only then can boats with their pennants ply the smooth surfaces of the water. Only then can lovers kiss in the oleander bushes. Only then can people be happy.

Brother Benda

Many centuries ago there was an Irish monk by the name of Benda. It had been quite a while since he lived in a monastery. Instead he would go from one place to the next and subsist on the generosity of others. Wherever he went, people were glad to see him and give him things. He was not only a guest in farmers' cottages and lowly inns but he was also frequently invited to dine with the lords in fortresses and castles and to contribute to their entertainment. You see, he was not a low-spirited person or a miserable wretch but a strapping fellow with large powerful hands and with feet capable of taking long steps and covering great distances. The womenfolk would look out the window and follow him with their gaze as he left and before he disappeared out the city gate or around the next bend in the forest path. They found it irritating that such a good-looking man wore women's skirts, and when he came back the following year, many of them blocked his way, trying unsuccessfully to rival the Virgin Mary. Benda did not try to stay clear of these seductresses; he didn't even look down in shame but looked them right in the eye, which immediately caused them to lower their gaze since they didn't get what they were after when this beam of pure human love was directed at them.

If the monk was an agreeable annoyance to the womenfolk in this respect, the same could occasionally be said of his effect on the men, who would have liked to provide him with arms and send him on a crusade. "Come along, Benda," they might say, plying him with wine and hearty fare. "We'll give you a horse, and you can lead a band of mercenaries. You are strong and vigorous and would make a good warrior, but you wouldn't do so well with your gift of gab." And then they drank with the monk to the voyage and the foreign countries, thinking they had won him over, only that in the end he mumbled he couldn't go along, he didn't have time; and the next morning he was nowhere to be found but had already left, not on a horse and in a white cloak but as a beggar and on foot.

This behavior was even more curious since the lords were absolutely right in their snide remarks about Benda's ability to express himself. The monk's strength was in his gaze, not in his tongue. He had a pleasant voice, but he was incapable of expressing what he felt. A stupid person then, the reader will think, and yet the opposite was true: a man whose emotions were stirred by a wealth of thoughts and a profusion of images, only that he never managed to put them all in order on the short distance from the conception in his mind to the birth in his mouth. But this order was most important to him; he had a definite idea of the power of ordered thought, an idea he expressed in his dull way to a fellow traveler here and there and to which he might have added that this particular order was God's real grace. He didn't seem to rely on this grace alone. Many people heard him mumbling to himself as he walked along, and when he had capably and diligently helped the peasants as compensation for his meals, he would probably sit down on a woodpile in the barn and practice, so that he gradually acquired a reputation for being in the process of preparing a sermon of a certain length and with a certain content. Since nothing ever came of the sermon and Benda just roamed the countryside, begging and mumbling to himself, he was probably also made fun of, in a good-natured way. "What's up, Brother Benda?" the men would say. "Is it time to ring the bells and sweep the village green? Would you like us to sound the drums and make room for the great orator before the Lord?" And they stopped laughing only when they happened to notice the deep sorrow in Benda's serene face as they said this.

Thus the years went by, and when Benda was about fifty years old, a considerable age in those days, people noticed that he got better at formulating his thoughts and that he spoke with greater ease. But this must have cost him enormous effort, or maybe you simply can't have both: experience and a pure childlike gaze. In any case, the gaze disappeared around this time. Benda suddenly had a vacant stare, and he would often stumble over every stone or drop things when women (no longer the young ones but the old ones) handed him bread. "Things are going downhill with Brother Benda," people would say, but that was not true. It was just that in time his eyes lost their radiance, and his legs would no longer carry him. He was no longer able to roam the countryside and had to content himself with finding shelter in a poor farmstead outside the village.

But he was not comfortable there. He talked incessantly to himself in his little room and pounded on the table. Yet when someone approached him, wanting to hear the word of God, which Benda was struggling with, he would suddenly grow silent and say "Go away, not yet, but soon; I'm not ready yet." Because he acted like that, and because he was an old man by now who didn't keep himself very clean anymore, he soon lost his friends. What could you feed a man of God, who didn't give you the least spiritual guidance, who refused to help out in the house, and who had even been sending the children away of late. After all, he had cared for them in the past because their parents, working hard themselves, left them to fend for themselves. "Go away, come back some other time, I don't have time," he would say to the children and to the grownups as well, usually women who looked him up so they could talk about themselves which, they thought, would be pure diversion and entertainment for a blind person. The women related how he had dismissed them with such unkind remarks that the children, who undoubtedly had been saddened but not offended by the phrase "no time," gradually lost all respect for the old man.

Benda's looks contributed to this, for his eyes developed an ugly, gray coating, which no one thought to cover up with a patch and which seemed as repulsive as greasy, grayish-green algae on a clear lake. "Slimy-Eye!" "Verdigris!" the children would shout after him, as he groped his way around the corner of the house into the open air, and they would even put a milk stool or a bucket of water in his way. In fact, it was probably such an obstacle that this careful and nimble blind man stumbled over one day when he fell down the narrow stairs. The result was that the farmer's wife had to bandage him and take care of him for a long time. In addition to all the other jobs she had to do, this one was disgusting to her, and so she decided not to allow the old man to go out. For safety's sake, for his safety's sake, as she said, she locked him up in his room and kept the key in her apron pocket. That way the children could only shout "Verdigris" and "Cross-Eyes" in front of his window, and the angry and fervent mumblings of the blind man responded in unholy fashion to the unholy prayer. The children soon found the singsong boring, and when they tried to come up with a better idea, they remembered what their parents had told them about a sermon he had never given. On the basis of this story they now devised a better plan, a plan that was at first simple but then became increasingly refined, and ultimately even devilish.

These children, whose desire to tease was to be Benda's destiny and ultimately his glory, were actually not children anymore. They were teenagers, fourteen and fifteen years old, three boys and a girl, who didn't come from the farm where the monk lived but from the surrounding area. There was no question of any criminal tendencies in any of them. They had simply grown up in bad times, nobody had assured them of their worth, and nobody had pointed out their potential. In their homes, mischief was the order of the day. They themselves were frequently the victims, now they wanted to get back at the adults and have a victim of their own.

For what they had in mind with the monk, they needed a dark, foggy day. Nobody was to do the job for them in the meantime in a fit of pity or from a wish to educate. "Let's just wait it out," Heinrich, the oldest, advised. "Wait till November, wait for rain, for early darkness." When Betty objected that the farmer's wife had less to do in late fall and that it therefore would be more difficult to get the key to Benda's room away from her, she was overruled and told they would soon find ample opportunity.

Little Kaspar, a real prankster by nature, was already practicing behind the granary where the road leads up to the rocky hillside and toward the cliffs. "Careful, this way, Brother Benda, there's a barbed wire fence, there's a ditch. Watch out, don't fall now!" The question was how they could make the blind man believe there were crowds of people waiting for him out there in the quarry, but clever Benno, Betty's brother, said he would come up with something in time.

The time arrived, an early, wet and foggy fall that is, and on a particularly unfriendly day there was indeed an opportunity not only to get the key but also to be alone in the house with the farm children, who had been clued in. The farmer was out chopping wood, and the farmer's wife was bringing him food. In the meantime the woman, who had never felt quite right about the whole thing in spite of her apparent insensitivity, had hung her apron on a nail in the kitchen. Coldly and methodically, the children started to carry out their plan. They posted sentries and listened in all directions to find out if anyone was coming near the farm. The dog, which normally would have barked, was in the woods with the farmers. When everything was still, the children went up the stairs to the room of the monk, who had been calmer in the last few days. When they unlocked the door from the outside and stepped into the room, which was already dark, Brother Benda was sitting very still at the table with a solemn look on his face. "I'm ready," he said, adding: "Are they there yet?" That confused the children somewhat since they thought they were giving the blind man a big surprise. Ill-mannered Heinrich with his pockmarked face stared at him, whereas ingenious Benno got hold of himself and said, "Yes, Your Excellency, they are already there waiting for you, a hundred people, no two hundred, three hundred. They are waiting for you in the quarry where the cliff forms a natural pulpit."

"'Your Excellency?'" Benda repeated astonished. "When did you start calling me that?"

"That's what they've always called you," little Kaspar said hypocritically. "You just didn't hear it because your mind was on something else."

"Everybody calls you that and talks about you the way they would about a saint," Betty said, ready to burst out laughing so that she thought it better to go ahead down the stairs, where the farm children, who had been posted as sentries, were motioning to her to be quiet.

Up above, Benda stood up. He asked to be allowed to wash himself and to put on his hooded robe, which took a lot of time, although he suddenly moved less clumsily and almost with the elegant agility of his youth.

"I was just wondering how they knew," he said, when the children opened the door. Then he put his hand on Heinrich's shoulder, so that

47

the boy almost collapsed, not from the burden but because he was ashamed and aware after all that they had to go through with this thing. Benno was already grinning at him, and little Kaspar spread out his coat and mocked the blind man with groping hands and laid-back head as he followed him toward the stairs.

"They all knew," answered Kaspar. "They are already ringing the bells, don't you hear them?" The Angelus, which announced that evening was coming, happened to sound just then. Since a blind man never knows what time it is, Kaspar could go ahead and add that it was now four o'clock.

"Nobody could have had any idea I would finish my work today," Benda said, "not even I knew that." He spoke in a deep, calm voice which itself sounded like a bell in the sounding of bells.

"Hurry up," said Benno, who was afraid the farmer and his wife would return, and he almost pushed 'His Excellency' in the back; but then he thought better of it and put his hand under his arm. So they went down the steep ladder and across the courtyard. Here Betty joined the little procession, but she did not allow the sentry to come with her, although he was all excited and wanted to go along.

As they went out the gate, Benda in the middle and still leaning on Heinrich's shoulder, the young people were almost frightened. That's how dark it had gotten, and suddenly it was so windy that the wet, black leaves of the trees in the alley hit them in the face and they stumbled on the slippery clay surface as if someone had tried to trip them. Maybe they would have liked to give up the whole thing at this point and under some pretense lead the blind man back to the house via a little detour. But they were ashamed in front of each other and became quite brave as they bragged about all the people they claimed to have seen out there by the quarry. A banner and the canopy under which they carried the bishop were also there. Their steps nevertheless became slower and slower, only that now it was the monk who, standing up straight and almost as if he could see again, picked up the pace and pulled the hesitant children along with him. A wild, enthusiastic smile covered his face, but now he listened dubiously to something in the distance, and soon he also raised the question they had feared: why you could hear neither voices nor steps from such a multitude.

"How can you hear steps," Benno said rudely, "when everyone is on his knees? How can they speak when they are covering their mouths with their folded hands? Afterward, when you are done with your sermon, you will hear all right how they shout with joy, praise God, and cry Hosannah." Because that's what they had planned. Benda would speak, in the meantime the children would retreat, and finally instead of a thousand voices the monk would hear nothing at all, not a sound, only dead silence. He would realize he had spoken before no one at all and that he had been deceived. For the present, however, the plan was to make him think they were just being silent. Therefore Kaspar and Betty remained behind for a little while, whispering and pulling Benno aside, too, and then the children jumped back and forth in the gray field, disguising their voices and playing their parts, something Kaspar was especially good at with his inventive cunning.

"Quiet now, there he comes, our dear master," he whispered in the voice of an old woman, while at the same time screeching like a three-year-old, "Pick me up, Daddy, I want to ride on your shoulders, I can't see." The others kept mumbling prayers and respectful greetings, now to the right, now to the left of the road, while pushing intruders out of the way in their own normal voices.

Whether or not Benda understood the deception was not entirely clear. It is possible he didn't hear any of it and was simply preoccupied with his own sermon, for he kept walking faster and faster at Heinrich's side. Soon they had reached the quarry, and the strangely shaped cliff that looked like a pulpit protruded from the foggy damp ground, gray and jagged.

"Careful, now, your Excellency," Heinrich said sincerely, forgetting that much worse things were to happen to the monk than hurting his foot on a piece of rock. They went down the mountain, the rocks were slippery and wet, but Benda moved with the uncanny confidence of a sleepwalker and reached his destination without paying any real attention to the shenanigans of the ghostlike voices. Standing in the pulpit, this man who so far had been silent, suddenly ordered quiet in a loud voice. He then extended his arms like someone hanging on a cross.

"Let's go," hissed young Heinrich, who had been with him until the last and who was eager to hide behind the cliff where the others sat making fun. The monk started to clear his throat, which sounded frightening and excruciating in the deep silence of the approaching night. Then he dropped his trembling arms and began.

I shall not render his sermon here. It is not written down anywhere, and I don't want to invent it. Besides, from what I have heard of it, I would never succeed anyway. For they tell me that in this address, which Benda had been preparing for so long and had revised countless times, no word was out of place, no expression missed its objective, and none of his imagery could have been more appropriate. Moreover, his language was certainly a far cry from ordinary bland but well-formed oratory; it was much more powerful and radiant and severe. Everything he had experienced on his wanderings and the way he had experienced it could be found in his sermon, not as a story but as conviction, maybe even just as a timbre of language, a rawness, a sweetness, a roll of thunder, a roar of the föhn. His topic was the salvation of man through love, but apparently it was not at all necessary to say so, because love was already there in his choice of words, and perfection was already there in his syntax. His thoughts did not come through in the form of pride or arrogance. He simply suspected that the moment of grace had come. Just this, he thought, and then to die out here in the quarry, to be raised and carried into the church and never again be back in that stuffy room.

The sermon was boring for the children, for everyone, that is, except little Kaspar. He suddenly began to listen, and it is probably to him we owe the preservation of this story. Little pranksters often turn into serious adults, and it is entirely possible that Kaspar still remembered and under-stood how to render the contents in his old age. But as I said, we don't have the sermon. We know only that the other children, who at first were poking each other in the ribs and giggling in the face of the emaciated, somber, flailing person in the pulpit, were also greatly distressed later on and finally dreaded the moment on which everything hinged, the moment at which the monk would speak his "amen" and everything would be still: no prayers, no rejoicing, no singing.

"You have been preaching to the rocks, Slimy-Eye," they had wanted to shout, intending to run away laughing, back home to their cozy rooms, whose windows were already brightly lit. They wanted to now as well, but without any real joy they held hands and were afraid. Because now it was night. It was night, and with the utmost difficulty the monk's voice brought his sermon to an end. It raised and lowered itself, wailed and threatened, and finally became gentle and mild. "And give you peace," said the monk, and then he breathed a deep sigh and added the word "amen" like a great peaceful exhalation.

"Now," cried Betty, even before his "amen." "Now we are going to get it."

"Now we will be torn asunder," Benno whimpered.

"Now the rocks will come tumbling down and take us with them," Heinrich prophesied, and by that they didn't even mean the monk but something much greater and much more terrible that they had offended in him.

But then they suddenly grew silent, bit their fingers, and beat their heads, because they thought they were dreaming or not quite in their right mind. You see, from down there, from the crowd of people, which was just make-believe after all, from the desolate, empty deep, came sounds of the most indescribable, wonderful harmony. It came closer and swelled to a chorus which sounded stronger and stronger, happier and happier, and even Benda seemed to perceive this, for when brave little Kaspar shone a torch in his face, he kept his head lowered in humility, smiled, and kept his eyes closed. All the while the singing went on and on down there, going right through your marrow because there was no one there who could have sung. Not even all the inhabitants of the town and all the peasants in the countryside combined could have sung like that, so powerfully and so purely.

It was the south wind, the parents said later, when the children came home, like squires carrying Benda, unconscious and dying, on his robe. But as long as they lived, the children never did believe it was the south wind that offered the blind monk gratitude and an answer to the endeavors of an entire lifetime.

The Everlasting Light

There are streets whose stories overpower you with their presence whether you want them to or not. Each archway and each window has its own story, each human being you run into has his. And until you've had enough, you don't even enjoy going for just an ordinary walk. It is afternoon, almost evening, clouds drift across the hill, spring is in the air. How wonderful it would be to have a cloak that would make you invisible, a wimple with white wings: Please don't talk to me, I'm not a human being with human ears; I'm a toad, jumping up to drink from the fountain of Sant' Onofrio; I'm a mangy little dog. How nice it would be to have peace and quiet away from all this human misery, to be alone and climb up there very slowly to watch the sunset from Gianicolo behind the stone pines of Villa Doria.

But Salita di Sant' Onofrio is not the kind of street that lets you enjoy your peace and quiet. No matter how tightly I close my eyes or fix my gaze straight ahead at the black stone oaks in front of the abbey, someone still insists on saying something to me. It is a woman, and now she even grabs my hand in an attempt to keep me from walking on.

"Won't you please come with me," she says, "for just a moment. Just up the stairs, you can't get in anyway, there's no room in the front hall, and besides the housekeeper doesn't allow it. Monsignor will have to come out on the landing to see you. But I don't want to be alone up there, don't you see?"

"Why don't you want to be alone?" I ask. "Everyone is alone, and of what use could I possibly be? I'm taking a walk right now; I'm a toad; I'm a mangy little dog."

But the woman who addressed me doesn't care. She won't let go of my hand but drags me with her into the house, the last house on the right in that street. I had almost reached the church, I had almost managed to get away. I'm still trying to free my hand, but the woman is strong, and she is still young. Her face reminds me of Rondanini's Medusa, but you should not think of her as a terrifying, spooky creature. The real Medusas were always beautiful and terrifying at the same time.

"What is it you want up there?" I ask. "Who is this Monsignor you keep talking about, and why don't you just go to church if you want to confess?"

52

"I don't want to confess," the woman says. "What I want is information. This is not the kind of place where you receive forgiveness for your sins. No, this is where you go for information." With these words she charges ahead of me across the marble floor. The walls along the stairs, too, are made of marble, but of course here in Rome that doesn't mean a thing. The smell of cats is so strong it almost makes you sick to your stomach.

"How long is it going to take?" I ask sternly. The woman says it can take quite a while, hours in fact, till it's our turn, but what does she mean by "our?" I don't even have any business here. All I had in mind was to see the sun set behind the stone pines of Villa Doria since it was already fairly low in the sky. But I soon realize the woman is right. We have to get all the way up to the sixth floor, but already by the fourth the line starts. There they sit on the steps, individually and in groups and whole families, chatting and moaning, and sometimes you notice a face drooping in a scarf like a dove in its cage, all white and still. Frau Medusa tries to push ahead past the people sitting on the lowest step, but they immediately hiss at her like adders, so she apologizes and stops. Then we too sit down on the cold, dirty marble, and I'm glad to be by a window with a cypress in front of it so I can look at its trunk and think about this fellow Linnaeus who once studied all the wild growth out there and put some order into it, albeit totally artificial but marvelous nonetheless. With human beings you just can't do that.

This Frau Medusa, for example, what is she really doing here, and what is it she keeps urging me to do? Why is she rambling on, and why is she so excited? I understand only this much: that she is talking about her husband and that this husband of hers never came back after the war, even though he is not dead.

"Here, take a look," Frau Medusa says, pulling a little picture out of her purse and blowing powder off it, strongly scented, cheap pink powder. It is a picture of a handsome young man, not in uniform but in a dark suit, tall, trim, good figure; and yet it isn't the figure but the face that is so striking. At first I don't even want to look at it. What do I care about Frau Medusa? What do I care about her husband? Why am I sitting here? Why do I reach for a strange photograph and hold it up to the light? Indeed, so much time has passed by now that you have to turn toward the window to be able to see well enough. But Frau Medusa is already yanking the picture away from me, kissing it, and putting it back in her purse. God really knows how to create beautiful human faces, masculine faces with nothing artificial about them, faces that contain all the elements of humanity: thoughts and feelings and sensuality and joy and pain. And all this poured into a mold worth looking at: high forehead, clear temples, strong nose,

LORETTE WILMOT LIBRARY
NAZARETH COLLEGE

chiseled chin. Much too good for Frau Medusa, I think. No, not too good. Frau Medusa, too, is something special with her black tangled hair and overly large sensuous mouth and her mortal ability to love.

Now she jumps up and drags me away from the steps. Three people are making their way down. Space has opened up all the way up, and it is possible to move forward, a few more feet, closer to the top floor.

"Monsignor sees everything," Frau Medusa says, sitting down again and pulling her skirt over her knees. "He knows where my husband is and whether or not he is in bed with another woman. For Monsignor is a dowser who knows how to locate the sources, and when he drops his pendulum above a photograph or a letter, the pendulum immediately starts to move, swinging back and forth or revolving around it. Monsignor may look at the pendulum, but he sees very specific things. This is not black magic, mind you, but a gift from the good Lord. Monsignor also knows exactly where the things occur that he happens to see there, how many kilometers to the north or to the south or to the east or to the west. All you need to do is go home and take a look at the map, and you are sure to find the village or the city."

If I don't see that? That one would want to get a man like that back? Frau Medusa begins to shout very loudly, and I understand it quite well. I would just like to get away, not to be present when Monsignor starts swinging his pendulum and the woman tears out of there. I already have a good idea of what she has in mind; I know it will mean deaths, at least one death, and all kinds of problems, certainly not happiness. It doesn't look as if there is any way of talking Frau Medusa out of it, I can't even get a word in edgewise. Why she dragged me along, I don't know. More and more people arrive. They are lined up all the way down to the street, and the air is bad. We've moved up two or three times. Right below me someone's broad, knit back shakes with sobs, and two little girls are clawing at the red wool, screaming máma, máma. I wonder what it is all these people want to know, most likely something they'd better not know. Or have they just lost their "fede," their wedding band, and Monsignor is supposed to find it, in the crack under the kitchen cupboard or under the chipped cup in the pantry? I haven't been able to see my tree trunk for quite a while. Oh well, it wasn't that comforting anyway, the kind of cypress whose wood twists upward, torn, splintered, spiraling, as if its growth had required extraordinary effort, prolonged agony. As I raise my head, I notice the door to the apartment standing open and, sure enough, here comes Monsignor, short and fat. He talks to a pale young man and makes the sign of the cross over him, then he thrusts a written message into his hand.

54

Frau Medusa has nudged me. She looks up ecstatically and quickly counts the people still ahead of us. There are nine or ten of them.

"We went to Assisi for our honeymoon," she says. "We went to the lower part of the church on Sunday. Everyone turned around and looked at my husband, and an Englishman took his picture. How lucky I am to have such a good-looking husband. I walk down the street, and I see him from the distance, so handsome and so proud, and my heart skips a beat because I know he is mine."

"You see him?" I asked surprised. Frau Medusa answers, "I don't see him. I am looking for him, he is somewhere, he is not dead."

"How do you know for sure?" I ask, not to be cruel but to prepare her a little, because now three more people come down the steps, their gaze lowered to the ground, their hands piously folded as if they were returning from the Last Supper.

"I know," says Frau Medusa, playing with a golden coin that is dangling from a chain around her neck. "A friend of his came home and swore on the Holy Bible it was true, but he didn't want to say anything more. I have no doubt there's someone behind it, a woman, I mean. There were soldiers who stuck around a place and got new papers and married and had children; and there are women, real hyenas who latch on to their husbands and devour the meat off their bones." Frau Medusa wanted to say even more about these hyenas, but now things are beginning to move on the steps. There's an old woman up there, who's not folding her hands piously but thrusting them above her head instead— horrible, bony, gnarled hands—screaming "che mondo assassino," which could mean, "What a murderous world this is," or better yet, "What a murder this world is," and then you picture the world as an evil giant harvesting the people off the street, putting them in a sack, and throwing the sack in the ocean the way you drown kittens. "Che mondo assassino," the old woman screams as she runs down the stairs with amazing agility. Here it's already dark, and wherever she passes someone, the people who are waiting jump up and scream hysterically. There are also some who are so frightened that they no longer care to know anything and don't want to stay around any longer, and therefore there is suddenly no one ahead of us anymore, only Monsignor standing in the doorway with a sad and bewildered expression on his face.

Frau Medusa has no intention of running away, of running back to happy ordinary life down there where one mingles with one's own kind. She rushes up the few steps to the top, and now she stands by Jacob's Ladder, where it smells like cooking, like stuffed peppers. Now she gets a little cardboard stub with a number on it out of her purse and, curtsying, hands it to Monsignor. Monsignor walks into the apartment, to his room;

then he comes out again and calls out down the empty stairs, "That's all for today." He motions for us to step inside, and because Frau Medusa has grabbed me by the arm, I go with her. But we are scarcely inside the narrow foyer before Monsignor opens another door and pushes me, just me, inside. It is a dining room with a long heavy table and a lot of black, straight chairs, and a window that's all sky with swallows swooping and swirling. It's airy in there, a real godsend after the stinking, narrow stairwell.

"I don't know anything about this, I don't have anything to do with her," I say, trying to explain how everything came about, but Monsignor has already closed the door behind him, and he and I are alone. Monsignor doesn't even listen to me. He urges me to sit down at the dining table, and he himself sits down next to me like the host at a solemn "pranzo." He places what looks like a menu in front of me, but it isn't a menu at all, this long, white sheet of paper. It is the message that Frau Medusa is to receive. That much I understand.

"So he actually did remarry, he did leave her?" I ask, and Monsignor stares at the long, white sheet of paper, shaking his head. It must be tiring, this dangling and gazing into the distance. Just think of all you get to see, nothing but problems and guilt. That can't be good for one, and Monsignor certainly doesn't look too well either, although his eyes follow the swallows and seem to be filled with happiness, usually, that is, but not now.

"There," he says, pointing to the paper. "That tells you what I have seen, and you can decide for yourself whether or not I should tell her." With these words he pushes the paper over in front of me, and I stammer, "I? What do you mean 'I'?" I begin to read: "We wish to confirm that F. C. ..." it says, and I visualize the little picture, this head of an archangel, this trim, vigorous figure. So, one more time: "We wish to confirm that F. C., born in Gennazzano in Latium and unaccounted for since the end of the war, is alive. He lives in a place surrounded by high walls, which apparently is located south of here, no more than a hundred and fifty kilometers away. The building is not a prison, not an insane asylum, and not a convalescent home. It is a refuge from the world."

"What do you mean 'a refuge from the world'?" I ask, because here the message ends. I look at Monsignor and worry because Monsignor does not look out the window or at me; in fact, he doesn't look at anything in particular.

"You don't know?" he says. "A spray of bullets, a ball of fire, a shower of phosphorous, and there is nothing left of a face, not even as much as death leaves for us. Then you're supposed to come home; the garland is already above the door, welcome home, brave soldier. But maybe something happened, maybe they gave you an artificial face made out of foam rubber, pink, but who wants to kiss it? You can't even shake hands because there is no longer a hand there to shake." Monsignor says all this in a low voice, but his words are like screams. "No one who looks like that would want to go home," he says, "because you can tolerate everyone except your loved ones. There are four or five such refuges for the maimed," he adds, "and Frau Medusa's husband is in one of them. She can look him up if she wants to."

If she wants to, I think, but then the door opens. Frau Medusa cannot have heard anything, but suddenly she is standing in the middle of the room, hammering at Monsignor's robe, right where his heart is supposed to be.

"I don't want to," she screams. "I don't want to be left out there. It's *my* husband, not *hers*. Tell me the truth. He's dead."

Monsignor steps back and looks at Frau Medusa as if he never saw her before, and maybe he never did see her. Maybe he just took the letter from her in the dark stairwell, a shadow among shadows. But now he does see her, now the great red evening sky is reflected in her face, and her features become clearly visible: her beautiful, firm cheeks, her radiant eyes, and her greedy, fleshy mouth.

"He is dead," Monsignor says, his head dropping on his chest.

"Swear it," Frau Medusa insists, "by the Holy Mary, Mother of God." But Monsignor doesn't do that. Instead, he falls on his knees between the sideboard and the table and begins to recite the death litany, and Frau Medusa, uttering a long deep moan, falls against the table.

"May the Lord God grant them eternal peace," Monsignor mumbles, "and may the Everlasting Light shine upon them." Before my eyes the men with the masks walk and creep through a garden full of wildly twisted and ragged cypresses, making strange gestures and bowing to each other while the swallows flitter across the sky above their heads.

I slip over to the door and hurry down the stairs. There is no one there anymore, and when I step outside, the darkness is already creeping up the steep alley. I don't walk up the hill at this point because the sun set long ago. I just linger in front of the house for a while until Frau Medusa comes down the steps. But she no longer recognizes me. Crying softly, her girlish face calm and still, she walks right over to the church.

The Miracle

What makes it so hard to communicate with Don Crescenzo is the fact that he is totally deaf. He can't hear a thing, and he's too proud to read people's lips. Neither can you start a conversation with him by writing something on a slip of paper. You just have to pretend that he's still like everybody else, that he is still a part of this noisy, garrulous world.

When I asked Don Crescenzo what things were like that Christmas, he was sitting in one of the rattan chairs at the entrance to the hotel. It was six o'clock, and the flow of afternoon traffic had stopped. It was perfectly still, and I sat down in the other rattan chair right under the barometer with the picture advertising the steamship company, a white ocean liner on a blue sea. I repeated my question, and Don Crescenzo put his hands up to his ears and shook his head apologetically. Then he got a notepad and pencil out of his pocket, and I wrote down the word "natale" and looked at him expectantly.

I'll get right on with my Christmas story, which is actually Don Crescenzo's story. But first I must tell you something else about Don Crescenzo. My readers should know how poor he once was and how rich he is now, a man in charge of a hundred employees, the owner of large vineyards and lemon groves and of seven houses. You will have to imagine his face, which seems more gentle with every year of deafness, as if faces were shaped and molded by the constant give and take of human discourse. Picture him walking around among his hotel guests, attentive and sad and very lonely. And then you should know that he likes to tell about his life and that he keeps his voice down rather than shouting when he talks to you.

I have listened to him often, and the Christmas story was familiar, of course. I knew it started with the night when the mountain came. Yes, that's what they had shouted: "The mountain is coming!" And they had yanked the boy out of bed and raced along the narrow mountain path. He was seven years old then, and whenever Don Crescenzo told about it, he put his hands up to his ears to let us know that that night surely was to blame for his present condition.

"I was seven years old and had a fever," Don Crescenzo said, raising his hands to his ears this time as well. "We were all in our sleep shirts, and that's all we had left after the mountain swept our house into the sea: the shirts on our backs, nothing else. Relatives took us in, and other relatives

58

gave us the property later on, the very same spot where the "albergo" now stands. My parents put up a house there even before winter arrived. My father did the masonry, and my mother hauled the stone down the slope to him in sacks. She was tiny and didn't have a lot of strength, and whenever she thought no one was near, she sat down for a moment on the steps and sighed, tears streaming down her face. By the end of the year the house was finished. We wrapped ourselves in blankets and slept on the floor, and froze a lot."

"And then it was Christmas," I said pointing to the word "natale," which is what I had written on the top sheet of paper.

"Yes," Don Crescenzo said, "then it was Christmas, and on that day I felt sadder than I had ever felt in my whole life. My father was a doctor, but one of those who don't write out bills. He went out and treated people, and when they asked what they owed, he said that first they had to buy medicine, then meat for their soup, and then he would let them know how much it would be. But he never told them. He knew the people here fairly well and was aware of the fact that they didn't have any money. He simply couldn't bring himself to remind them, even right after we had lost everything and our last savings had gone for the construction of the house. He tried it once shortly before Christmas, the day we had used up the last wood in our stove. That evening my mother brought home a stack of white slips of paper, and my father jotted down the names on the slips with a couple of figures by each one. When he was done, he got up and tossed the slips in the fire, which was just about to go out. The fire flickered very beautifully, and it made me happy, but my mother winced and looked sadly and angrily at my father.

So it was that on the twenty-fourth of December we had no more wood, no food, and no clothes that were fit to go to church in. I didn't think my parents gave it a whole lot of thought. When things like that happen to grownups, they have no doubt things will turn out all right in the end and that they will be able to eat and drink and praise the Lord again as they have done so many times over the years. But for a child it's another matter. A child sits there waiting for a miracle, and when the miracle doesn't occur, all is lost ..."

As he said this, Don Crescenzo leaned forward and looked out in the street as if something out there were claiming his attention. But actually he was just trying to hide his tears. He tried not to let on how the venom of disappointment still permeated every pore of his body to this day.

"I'm sure our Christmas is very different from the kind of Christmas they have where you come from," he continued after a while. "It's a very noisy, very happy occasion. In the procession the infant Jesus is carried in a glass shrine, and a brass band plays. Mortars are fired for hours on end, and the sound of the shots reverberates from the rocks so that it sounds like a mighty battle. Rockets shoot up in the air, turn into gigantic palm trees, and drift down into the valley in a shower of stars. The children scream and yell, and the ocean with its black wintry waves roars so loudly it's as if it were crying and singing with joy. This is our Holy Night, and the whole day is spent preparing for it. The boys set up their little fireworks, and the girls make wreaths and clean the silvery fishes that they adorn the Madonna with. In every home the women are roasting and baking and making sweet syrup.

That's the way it had been in our family as long as I can remember. But on the Christmas Eve that followed the landslide, it was terribly still in our house. There was no fire, and therefore I stayed outside as long as I could, because it was always a little warmer out there than inside. I sat on the steps looking up toward the street where people walked past and where wagons with their weak little oil lamps came and went. There were lots of people about, peasants on their way to church with their families and others who still had something to sell—eggs and live poultry and wine. As I sat there, I could hear the cackling of the chickens and the happy chatter of the children who were telling each other what all they would experience later that night. My eyes followed each wagon until it disappeared in the dark hole in the tunnel, and then I turned my head and looked out for the next vehicle. When the street got less noisy, I thought the festivities had started and I would now hear the boom of rockets and cries of enthusiasm and joy. But all I heard was the sound of the ocean crashing against the rocks and the voice of my mother praying and asking me to join her in the litany. I finally did, but quite automatically and without my heart being in it. I was starved and wanted to eat—meat and sweets and wine. But first I wanted my festivities, my wonderful festivities ...

Then suddenly everything changed in the strangest way. The footsteps on the street no longer went past, and the vehicles stopped. In the glow of the lamps, we saw a full sack being thrown into our garden and baskets piled high being placed along the side of the street. A load of firewood and kindling came rolling down the stairs, and when I groped my way up the steps, I found on the lower little wall plates and dishes filled with eggs, chickens, and fish. It was quite a while before the mysterious sounds stopped and we could see how rich we suddenly were. Then my mother went into the kitchen and made a fire, and I stood outside eagerly inhaling the aroma that comes from this blend of sizzling oil, onions, minced chicken, and rosemary.

At that moment I didn't know what my parents might have already suspected: that my father's patients, those old debtors, had decided to make him happy this way. For me it was manna from Heaven—the eggs and the meat, the glow from the candles, the fire from the stove, and the beautiful smock that I fished out from a bundle of clothes and put on as fast as I could. "Run," said my mother, and I ran down the street and through the long, dark tunnel, at the end of which colored lights were already glowing and sparkling. As I came into town, I could see from far away the red and golden canopy under which the bishop was carried up the steep steps. I heard the drums and the kettledrums and the cries of "evviva," and I joined in the shouting with all my might. And then the big bells started to sway and hammer away in their open tower."

Don Crescenzo fell silent and smiled happily to himself. Surely he heard again now, with his inner ear, all these wild and booming sounds which had been silent for him for so long and which meant even more to him in all his loneliness than to any other human being: love of his fellow man, love of God, the rebirth of life out of the darkness of the night.

I looked at him, and then I picked up the notepad. "You ought to write, Don Crescenzo. Your memoirs." — "Yes," Don Crescenzo said, "I should." For a moment he sat up straight, and you could see he valued his own life story no less than the stories in the *Old Testament* or the *Odyssey*. But then he shook his head. "Too much to do," he said.

Suddenly I knew what he was up to with all this remodeling and new construction, with the bar and the garages and the elevator down to the beach. He wanted to shield his children from hunger, from unhappy Christmas Eves, and from the memory of a mother hauling sacks full of stone so that she finally had to sit down and weep.

Home Alone

Everyone keeps asking me how it all came about recently, the day before All Souls Day, and why I did what I did. After all, it wasn't the first time I was home alone for a couple of hours. You'd think I'd be used to it, they say. It was a gloomy day all right, but not a particularly nasty one, and there was plenty to eat, fried potatoes and even a chunk of sausage. My mom always mentions that piece of sausage when the subject of this unlucky day comes up, which happens fairly often. And every time she lets me know what a good sausage it was, calf liver sausage, she says, that cost an arm and a leg, and there were also a couple of apples and a banana and some Pfeffernüsse in a bag on the kitchen counter. I had always been allowed to eat whatever I wanted, nobody would ever have come down on me for that. Besides, they don't see why I didn't just get out of there if I minded being alone, why I didn't go down to the courtyard or visit the kids on the ground floor, or even go to the movies. It would have been all right to go to the Alhambra on the corner, where a movie was showing that wasn't restricted. After all, I had enough spending money; they wouldn't have minded at all.

Really, I could have done any of these things, or I could have plopped down on my bed and slept until my parents got home from work, because I was beat that day. I clearly remember yawning a couple of times on the stairs and putting my hand over my mouth very fast several times, which makes such a funny sound. The stairwell was kind of dark, as it always is at this time of year. Only the water sprite in the stained glass pane still shone a little. You don't see things like that anymore, but our building is pretty old. It was quiet, too, nobody coming up or down the stairs, only on the third floor behind the door to the right I could hear a dog growl. "You filthy mongrel, you nasty old mutt," I whispered, because I knew it hated that more than anything. Then I yelled bow-wow real loud and raced down the stairs because this great big hideous beast had been known to jump up and depress the door handle. But that day it didn't jump up, and it didn't bark either. In fact, it stopped growling right away, and I still remember I wasn't too happy about that. So I yawned again and slowed down while unbuttoning my jacket and pulling out the house key, which my mom had tied around my neck on a piece of string that morning although I could just as easily have stuck it in my pants pocket.

As I unlocked the door and stepped into the hall, I noticed a stuffy smell, and I knew right away that the beds hadn't been made again. I guess nobody had had time before they left. I was right. The breakfast dishes were still on the table, even the butter and the bread. So the first thing I did was put the butter in the refrigerator. Then I went into the bedroom and straightened the sheets a little and pulled the covers up over them because I know my dad has a fit every time he comes home and things look a mess. As a matter of fact, they had argued about that several times, and my dad, who is always so uptight, yelled a lot. But my mom just laughed and said, "Well, I guess I could stay home, but you'd soon see what that's like when they come and haul the stereo and the refrigerator away. And just who was it that wanted that car anyway, you or I?" But then she was suddenly very nice. She stroked my dad—and me, too—and she said once we got the car, the three of us would drive out in the woods and have a picnic and play tag. It would even be okay with her to kick the football around. But that never happened, because when they finally did get the car, they always invited their friends out, grownups who didn't feel like walking anywhere, and the trails in the woods were closed to cars. That didn't bother me a whole lot though, I've been carsick too many times for that.

I have always wished my mom would get sick again, like the time she sprained her ankle and I made arnica poultices for her and brought her coffee in bed. I've often wondered how I could finagle it so that she would get a real stomach ache. But she never did get a stomach ache. In fact, she has always looked pretty healthy, and she's often said she enjoys going to the office because there are people around and it's so boring to be home all day. Besides, she's not too tired when she gets home, and she is always game when my dad wants to go to the movies. The one thing she can't stand is party games, and she says reading aloud is too hard on her because she has to look at print and handwriting all day long. So I have to read my books by myself because, after all, I'm a big boy now. I'm a big boy all right, and of course I can read my books by myself. Besides, I always have lots of homework, only on that particular afternoon I didn't have any because two of my teachers were gone. Instead I had to straighten the beds, and when I was done with the beds, I should really have warmed up some leftovers. I was hungry all right, otherwise I wouldn't have yawned so much. But suddenly I didn't feel up to it anymore, so I just stuck a couple of cold potatoes in my mouth; then I was going to go right in and play.

Later on all the grownups wanted to know what my favorite toys were. It would have made sense to them if I had said the long ladder on the fire engine or the doll house, which has a tiny advent wreath with genuine little candles on it. In short, anything that had to do with fire or with light. Instead I said I liked to play with my miniature cars, whose garage is underneath the cupboard. The parking attendant is a little soldier in a brown uniform, which I once found in a pile of rubble, and every time my dad sees him, he tells me to get rid of that damned SA officer. But I hold on to him because I need him and because I don't have the faintest idea what a damned SA officer is anyway. Not that I really wanted to play with my cars that afternoon. What I really wanted to do was play with my "family," but my parents don't know anything about this, and there is no need for them to know about it either. That goes for my teachers as well, and certainly for the doctor, whom my parents refer to as "uncle doctor" in front of me, although they never had any dealings with him before and don't ever know how to act when he's around.

"Well, so you were playing with your cars?" the so-called uncle doctor said, making a strange face. I nodded and looked at him as if he had two heads, thinking to myself: I wonder what he would have to say about my family, I mean about the fact that my dad is an old football by the name of Popp and my mom is a funny doll without legs by the name of Mingel and that she has two other children besides me, one of whom is an old chess piece while the other is a partly deflated balloon.

I keep this entire family hidden in a box in my toy chest, and when I get home from school, I take them out and put them in their chairs, and then I go out in the hall again and act as if I were just getting home. As soon as I step into the room, my family starts laughing happily.

"Well, well, here is our youngest," says Popp, who is sitting in his armchair, making a friendly full-moon face. And Mingel says, "Come over here, my boy," stretching out her arms with the sawdust leaking out. "How were things on the prairie today?" asks my brother Harry, the chess piece made of ivory. "Great," I say, and then I start telling about all the wild mustangs I caught with my lasso, making it so exciting that my sister Luzia, the balloon, begins to wiggle with excitement.

"I bet you'll want some of this good bear stew," Mingel says, and because she doesn't have any legs at all, I have to carry her over to the stove where she immediately starts to stir something in a pot. In the meantime I go out on the balcony with my brother and show him the moon rocket which is flying over the rooftops just now, and we take bets on whether it will finally make it today or burn out beforehand, as it has been known to do. Then we write our names on little slips of paper, which means we are volunteering for the next flight to the moon. We hide these slips of paper under a flowerpot because Popp and Mingel are always so worried about us and would never allow something like this. All day long they sit at home waiting for us, and we are no sooner back in from the balcony before they ask if it is foggy out there and if we caught cold. "Of course not, why would we catch cold?" we say, our voices sounding pretty raw. Then we sit down at the table, and I tease my sister and tell her she is getting thinner and thinner and losing her color.

"Leave her alone," says Popp, and then we discuss what to do next, and I get the horse race out of the closet.

Whenever we play this game, Mingel always wants the white horse, but she never has any luck with the dice, and I sometimes have to cheat a little and fix it so that she, too, gets to win once in a while. Popp doesn't care if he wins or not. He rolls around on his chair and says, "Mingel, what would we do without our kids!" Then Mingel starts to cry a little—she is so sentimental—and Luzia has to comfort her and chat with her about the Christmas cookies.

That's the way it was every day when I got home from school, and you can see why I didn't want to go down to the courtyard or play with those nasty kids on the first floor who always fight and can't open their mouths without saying "shit" or "crap" every chance they get. And, of course, I wasn't interested in playing with these guys who always whistle up at my window and make fun of me because I won't join their gang and because they think I'm too good for them or too cowardly. Of course I'm not a coward. I just never felt like it, and time always went by so quickly. In the middle of the most wonderful game, I would hear my mom or my dad open the front door, and I would just have time to quick put my family away and open up my textbooks. But on the afternoon before All Souls Day, I didn't have to open any books or put my family away in a great hurry, because they weren't there to start with. The whole family was gone, simply wasn't there.

When I first sat in front of my toy chest trying to get the box out and I didn't find it right away, I just figured it was in the bottom drawer or in the wardrobe or wherever. Things always had to go so fast, and I don't always watch what I'm doing. So I started a major search: inside the cupboards, underneath the cupboards, and finally even on top of the cupboards, where I couldn't reach at all. I had to get up on the good silk chair in my dirty shoes, which really upset my mom afterward. Finally I went back to the toy chest, and then I suddenly noticed the cardboard box, but in a totally unlikely place, and when I opened it, it was full of old dominoes. Now I was really suspicious. I ran into the kitchen and opened the trash can, which is brand-new with something like a gas pedal that you just need to step on to open the lid. But there was nothing in the trash can, only a few potato peelings and a lot of crushed silk paper. I yanked it out and tossed it on the gas stove, and later they asked me why, but I didn't tell them. I kept searching all afternoon long. If my things were not in the trash can, they had to be somewhere else. Somewhere! That meant opening all the other drawers and searching through all the shelves, not to mention the linen closet and the sideboard. I got more and more upset, much more than I would be over an old football, a broken doll, a chess piece, or a deflated balloon. I didn't doubt for a moment that I was acting crazy, and for a split second I thought of naming some other objects Popp and Mingel and Harry and Luzia and in a certain sense building a new family this way. But I felt instinctively that I wouldn't do that anymore, because I guess I was much too old for that sort of thing. When I finally stopped looking and stood there in the kitchen by the window, I knew that from then on I would always be as lonely as I feel right now. Because I hadn't gotten around to turning on the light, it was already dark in the apartment and so awfully deserted and still. At that point, I felt I couldn't take it any longer. I wanted to get away, to the movies on the corner. I had enough spending money after all, and I guess I wouldn't refuse anymore if they should come around and ask me to join the gang, even though the guys in the gang insist on doing really crazy stuff like slashing tires and smashing store windows. I guess they don't have anything better to do. But maybe in time I might take a liking to that sort of thing, and in any case I wouldn't be so lonely anymore.

I thought about all this and stayed there by the window next to the gas stove, and that's how I got the idea of lighting the burners, all four of them, not to warm up my meal, really just sort of for fun. So I removed the four covers and turned all the burners on the highest setting. The flames were so high and cheerful and bright and warm, and I was happy and thought it might even be possible to talk to the flames. But as luck would have it, all that silk paper from the trash can was lying on the stove, and it must have caught fire and spread to the curtain. Whatever, it was suddenly in flames that reached to the ceiling, and I got scared and screamed for help. Fortunately my dad was just unlocking the front door, but then all this questioning started right after that and this bit about my teacher and the doctor, as if I weren't quite right in the head or as if I had been mad at my parents. I mean, my mom couldn't have had any idea what she had thrown out or given away. I don't really have anything against my parents at all. They are the way they are, and actually they are okay. It is just that there are certain things you can't share. All you can do is write them down and then tear them up again when you're home alone.

It's getting dark now, and down below the guys in the gang are whistling for me. In just a few minutes I'll open the window and let them know I'm on my way. Then I'll swagger down the stairs, my hands in my pockets, past the water sprite that I used to like so much. And suddenly conscious of the fact that I'm not a kid anymore.

Circe's Mountain

Friday

Here underneath the fig tree one could begin to live again! This means one thing to one person and another to someone else, but in my own case it means to love and to write. I don't mean the act of writing itself, of course, which is hard work, but rather a special way of looking and listening, with the idea in mind of telling a story. Here underneath the fig tree, one day after a breakfast of pitch-black espresso, tiny eggs, and bread without butter. When Felice has stopped his tricycle behind the hedge and called "Oggi tutto a posto?" which is an elegant way of offering his ware, he hopes, of course, we will rush out and buy baskets full of tomatoes and beans and hard, green peaches, all the while adamantly refuting his question. When the garbage truck comes by, raising lots of dust, and we have forgotten to put out the can as usual and have to run after the truck in a cloud of dust, the men have already stopped and are walking back toward us, laughing goodnaturedly. In the morning, when irresistible Mauro turns the corner and parks his Vespa in the shade by Pozzo's, sometimes with a friendly greeting and sometimes without saying anything at all, you can read on his face how things went on the dance floor the night before, whether Costanza was nice to him or ignored him, or whether she took off with the engineer for the beautiful, mysterious hotel at the foot of the mountain or for the Temple of Jupiter in the moonlight. He knows what goes on there all right. As a matter of fact, Costanza and Annamaria were up there last night, but at the critical moment Costanza did her inimitable routine, the whiny voice and what did he mean "bella luna?" After all, there were neither stars nor fishing boats to be seen, and she was freezing, it was cold. Then they drove home, and twice there was a black cat by the roadside, and each time the engineers, these grown men, stopped the car, shifted into reverse, and backed up to the nearest crossroad to drive home on the tricky, bad roads, anything to avoid going past the cat. The girls go on about this as they lie there in the hammock and in the deck chair, stretching and refusing to start the day with flute practice and vocabulary drill. Their voices are like breakers that come and go, wishing to pull me along with them, back into life. My own night was long and restless, a constant tossing and turning on my crisp straw mattress, a mental walk along the beach, along the edge of the waves where the sand is wet and hard, past the walls of reeds, past the entrance to the caves, always looking for a body, for your long, slender, youthful body, washed ashore by the sea, washed ashore by death, for the sea is also death. I wanted to embrace this body and awaken it, yet not awaken it, just embrace it, because this decomposure in the ground, this turning into bone, is the worst thing of all. What do bones mean to us? "Did you have a bad night?" Annamaria asks, and Costanza says it's the moon's fault; the moon on the ocean is dangerous. Then she jumps up and curses the dirty-white chicken we call Candida, which struts past us every morning into the dining room, leaving something black and damp behind. Sighing, Annamaria clears the table, and Costanza goes up to her room from where we soon hear the first sounds of her flute, monotonous, harsh, and unpleasant, played solely for practice.

Saturday

It starts with my eyes, which have been refusing to see: no colors, no shapes, only a gray blur, eyes that don't care to see anything either, since your eyes are gone and decomposed, and every glance and perception is an act of survival, and survival is betrayal. For let no one remind me of the fairy tale about the jug of tears, of this dead child who pretends to suffer when its mother fills the jug to overflowing with her tears. That fairy tale is nothing but an invention by survivors anxious to experience life, by those who are sick of crying and who don't want to imagine how lonely the dead are, how terribly alone. But those who do imagine that have black moss growing over their retina that swallows up everything, and their ears are so completely shut that they can't hear life's siren sounds, which are not necessarily beautiful music but maybe just the braying of a donkey in the withering field of artichokes or the barking of dogs at night. Nevertheless, it starts one day. The eyes do see again, possibly here in San Felice, the image of Circe, a head made out of rock, lying there, thrust back, gazing into the merciless sun. An enormous profile against the southern sky, Circe turned to stone like Niobe, like all desperate human beings, Circe who for all her magic could not hold on to Odysseus or cure his longing for Ithaca, for death. It was the head of Circe that I noticed today, naked, terrible, and beautiful above the cork oak forests of Torre Paola. After that, it made no difference that some lively friends of ours came down from Rome that night and abruptly transferred the legend to the Black Sea: Circe, Odysseus, his transformed companions, all of them at the Hellespont. My eyes were suddenly open anyway, no more black moss on the retina, no more thoughts of betrayal, and just enough tears to cover the soft colors of the adventurous sea with a glaze of mother-of-pearl.

Sunday

Willingly or unwillingly I am most likely on my way back—back, from where? From a state of numbness, indifference, petrification—a road that resembles the subterranean passage between Lakes Avern and Cumae, whose darkness sometimes is penetrated by light falling through shapeless holes in the vaulted ceiling, light which also means vistas, vistas of laurels and lemons and the branches of fruitbearing orange trees, a real vista of life and paradise for the Northern European who is all too familiar with the path between underworld lake and sibyl's grotto. The path back to reality, except that where we live there are neither laurels nor lemons nor fruitbearing orange trees. You see, we live on the plain, from which the rock juts out as sharply as the fist of the man who was buried alive, the one who was discovered by our neighbor one night (by full moon, of course) and which I'll tell you about some other time. A fist, a hand, a fan, and on the slope toward the ocean the flora of southern isles, the natural flora of macchia and olive groves and the cultivated one of roses and geraniums and showy bougainvillea with shrub oaks in the gorges and orange trees and grapes in the shade of the rock walls. But as I said, except for the fist, the fan, there was none of that, no sign of Klingsor's enchanted garden, only flat land, dusty-white roads, salt and dust-encrusted kitchen gardens, artichokes, and fields of grain. The barley is being harvested right now, not with threshers, not even with scythes, but with sickles, short-handled knives curved as the moon, as it always has been. Sickles, men with sickles who suddenly pop up from their bent positions, with eyes burning in their deeply tanned, sweaty faces, asking the girls what time it is and running after them so that Costanza and Annamaria jump aside with fear and call back over their shoulders again and again "l'una e mezza." Rushes and reeds and eucalyptus trees, cool and slender with their silvery, slightly wavy leaves, which hang close to the trunk and cover the ground around it, the color of flesh and lilac, a pleasant decay without pathos, without stiffening and flaming anger. That's what it looks like here where we live, around our little house and as far as the eye can see, and the public beach between here and Terracina is a disorderly desert strewn with litter. Once in a while some boys are there playing soccer in the late afternoon between the water and the walls of reeds, and a little horse pulls a cart loaded with iron rods at the edge of the shore. The black, sluggish canals from the interior carry the smell of swampland, melancholy, and autumn into the salty freshness. What else can I tell you, silent heart, and do you even want to hear it, do you even want to know?

Monday

Eyes, new eyes for Costanza, for her calm, measured movements, for the unspeakable purity and integrity of her gaze. Like someone who has returned from a long trip, I find she has suddenly come of age; my darkness was a beneficial shade for her, my dullness a ritardando, which allows us to keep pace with one another instead of my running ahead and pulling her behind me as I did when she was little. Fear, this constant, burning parental fear of neglecting something, of leaving something important unsaid, has diminished. Because I know that I have only her, I also know that I don't have her anymore, that I must not demand anything of her, not even an understanding of my crippled condition, my self-hatred. I must conceal the fact that I belong to you, a dead man, and therefore to death itself. She is not to hear any more about our love, about this unique bond between two people, which must finally seem like something horrible and inhuman to her. For after all, the wheel has turned once: fall, winter, spring, summer; it has been a long time, and a daughter, of all people, must find her own way. Each generation has its own way of living and loving or of not loving, or of waiting, and ultimately a mother must realize, difficult as it is, that that too has some validity, this gradual easing back into life, this being at home in the most inhuman of the arts: music. One of these days she will have to listen to the flute passages and realize how strange and yet familiar every child is in its fears and threats, in its love for life and longing for death. That and everything else that has a bearing on Costanza's case: the demonic waters of the Danube and your ride on horseback across Poland in a tattered uniform; my walks through the vineyards and the beech forests of the Breisgau; and the last Schnävelin, the dwarf.

Tuesday

The moon, which they talk so much about in San Felice, this disturber of sleep and kindler of love, is rising over the ocean, a circular opening in the wandering firmament, a hole in the back of which a gentle fire burns. Only later does it become large and silvery, spreading its light across the water before disappearing on the other side of the mountain, so that it is already behind us and only the fishermen out there can see its broad trembling beam of light on the waves.

Sitting on the terrace at Cartuzza's with my feet resting on the balustrade, I watch it sleepily, incapable of believing that someone soon will be going up there, that cool Selene is being readied for the warlike enterprises of our own planet. They also watch it or talk about it on television in the little hotel lobby. There the bleary-eyed children sit, tiny in the big chairs, glued to the set. On the screen, too, there are constantly children, some with their mothers, children of men who will soon be put in capsules and fired off to the moon. Wow, says the patronizing television reporter, aren't you proud that's your dad? Clutching their toys, the children say they are very proud and just can't wait. Their well-groomed mothers are proud, too, each one hoping that her husband will get there first. Ladies and gentlemen, your attention, please—and all over the world people are holding their breath. Wives of heroes, children of heroes, and out there cool Selene again, just a bit higher, bathes the woodlands and the valleys, even in the Black Forest. As I sit there staring at the moon, the disc of the dance floor rises toward it, round and silvery, rises with all the dancing couples above the white-flowering oleander, above the tops of the mimosas and the pepper trees and the straw-thatched roof of the bar. A melancholy tune follows the transported dancers, exhorting a young murderer to "hang down his head and cry." Then it stops, and the lights go out. The wind springs up, the iron poles clang, and sand drifts across the terrace.

Wednesday

Ears, new ears for the stories you hear around here. The one about the man who was buried alive, for example, which I heard about in all its gory detail at the beauty parlor today. My hairdresser knows everything about it. The hero, the same one who raised his fist, was his cousin, and he also knew the other people in the story, of course, pale, beautiful Nanna, who became the cousin's sweetheart and lived with him and grew flowers in tin cans on his terrace, all of them fiery red—fuchsias and geraniums and salvias—and who wore a necklace of thick black wooden beads. "Ehi, Nanna," his bricklayer cousin would call from afar when he came home from work at night gunning his motorcycle. Then Nanna's white face would peer out from among the flowers as young Gianni disappeared down the stairs and out the backdoor. The cousin didn't notice anything; but isn't someone who never notices anything worse than someone who looks around and beats up the next guy? Isn't he really disgusting in his self-assurance and pride of possession? Isn't he really asking for trouble? Isn't he really taking a knife to his own guts? Young Gianni spends late afternoons with Nanna. In the evening she throws him out, and he goes to the movies to watch the knifings, the stranglings, and the shots from the hip, whatever it takes to silence a man who doesn't talk that much in the first place. The fact that he may actually have loved his rival even more than the girl is an observation of the hairdresser's. It engaged him to such an extent that he stopped working on my hair, lit a cigarette, and blew the smoke at the dim mirror while he told his story. "I guess that's probably why he did such a sloppy job," I say, pondering for my part the Italians'

71

love of men, of women, of humanity as a whole. The hairdresser throws his cigarette in the washbowl and states the facts: how Gianni and Nanna put the dead cousin on the motorbike, strapping his arms around Gianni's chest while Nanna got on behind with the shovel across her knees. For now the body had to be hidden, then buried, but most of all hidden, because there was no point in throwing it in the ocean. The ocean doesn't keep anyone; it washes off the blood but doesn't close the wounds. Therefore they buried him quickly, a botched-up job, in the soggy soil, far away from the vineyards of the village, down there on the plain where the tourist cottages are. Buried it, but not deeply, as if they didn't really care. He could thus perhaps have surfaced, but they surely had no idea he would have started to himself. "I think I'd better get under the dryer," I say when my hairdresser has gotten to this point in his story, and I'm already reaching over myself to cram the humming shell over my head, because this story is getting too close for comfort. In my neighbor's yard, there is nothing but black fists sprouting among the Roman chamomile. And, of course, there was no help for the cousin. There is no help for any of us, not for you or for me, we are all in the hands of fate.

Thursday

To write, to describe, to create a world of my own—I wonder what makes me start doing it again. Because I can't live in a darkness without form, or because I want to remind you of all the things that were so precious to you here, the landscape you loved as the theater of human desire and restlessness, but also as an act of creation, as stone and wall and herb. Those who are able to see things from above surely must long for what is small and close up, just as passengers in an airplane under whose feet the puzzling mosaic of the earth's surface is pulled along suddenly long for the putrid smell of harbors or want to crumble some rain-soaked earth in their hands or rest their foreheads in prickly grass. Since there is nothing else I can give you anymore, I want to give you this: Ristorante Cartuzza, a bar in a straw-thatched hut, a jukebox, bushes and trees and faded canvas umbrellas, all of these things, toy-size in my hand and now erected for you between the road and the sea. Then there are the little chairs, red and white wooden chairs that I set up, tiny ones, but mustn't everything be tiny for your eyes now, toys for the giant? And the farmer with his plow, the horses, the girl giant and the scolding father giant, they are all dead. Toys for a giant, this summer beach, this bit of life for two short months, not to mention the special game: the glass-covered case in which a ball rolls down the slanting surface between bright, bell-clanging obstacles and suddenly flashing lights, the ball wanting to hide in the black hole. But there is a lever that erects two small barriers at just the right moment, and that's what the game is all about: to get the ball back into the labyrinth, back to the little columns and flashing lights, no rest, no rest for a long time. Above the case, numbers are registered on a board: Winnings? Years of one's life? And then there is the glass automat that swallows coins and advances small records until they drop in place, "When you Smile at me, Giulia" and "Catch a Falling Star." But it's only June, it's too early for falling stars. Finally there's the flagpole on Cartuzza's terrace and the signal light with which the young waiters—children in long pants and white jackets—send their playful messages at night when the excursion boat returns from Ponza: short, short, long, long. From far away, out of the white twilight, indistinguishable from sea and sky, someone signals back.

Friday

In the morning everything seems neat and orderly on the beach, and yet it isn't, not even the activities of the children. The kids are playing very nicely with their little buckets and shovels, but if you look at them with the sensitive eyes of someone who is surprised at every turn, the eyes of someone who has been blind for a long time, they soon take their place in the masked dance of human passions, which they perform with grace and mystery. Beach games, sand games, the big ocean barely plays a role although it is shallow far out. This was apparent the first evening we were here, when Annamaria took off her shoes and raised her skirt and slip to her waist, as all the young men watched her wade through the black water under the stars to catch the dinghy of the motor boat, a harebrained idea, a stubborn impulse that contributed to the notion that my daughters were crazy.

But they are not the ones I want to talk about. I want to talk about little Nina with her chubby, red face whose sole occupation is going and getting buckets of water. Holding a large comb in her left hand, she puts her bucket down and switches the comb to her right hand. First she combs her mother's hair and then her father's, her big brothers', her aunts', and their girlfriends', while occasionally dipping the comb in the water and then getting more water as needed. Finally the whole family refuses, but the people under the next umbrella are game. All morning long she does nothing but comb and smooth (one more time, one more time!), with her fat little hands and her red, dead-serious face.

I must also mention Peppino, who insists on burying his mother in the sand. He puts sand on her legs and pats it down (the toes, these awful animals); sand on her arms, sand on her stomach and on her chest, which rises and falls so that there are constantly cracks, sand on her neck and her hair, until nothing more is left than a little, spooky triangle with rolling eyes and gasping lips. Peppino is frightened and about to run away, but

73

then his mother breaks through her cover laughing. Stamping his feet, Peppino screams "one more time, one more time" until she lets him.

Then there is Joan, a little English girl, six years old with a loud, hoarse voice and jerky movements. She hides underneath the beach towel, and the grownups know perfectly well what to do and what to say: "I wonder where Joan is?" followed by far-fetched speculations: in Africa on top of an elephant, at the North Pole on an ice floe. For the longest time Joan doesn't stir; then finally she is overcome with homesickness and pulls the beach towel off her head. Sometimes she gets it all twisted; she can't breathe and she rolls around in a circle, a blue and red bundle of toweling. "Here is Joan," she finally screeches, consoling and triumphant, her rosy face peering out from its frame of wet curls, and already she reaches for the cover again, the magic cloak of invisibility (one more time, one more time), only to start the game all over again.

Oh yes, and the little boys who jump off the lighted terrace down to the beach at night, ten feet down to the naked, moonlit sand where the umbrella stands rise like shattered tree trunks in a totally foreign landscape. They have to throw down their little red sandals first so there is something there waiting for them. But no sooner have they landed before they slip on their shoes and head for the stairs to stand up there one more time and feel the shudder of fear, as their clenched hands let go of the balustrade one more time and they jump, one more time, one more time ...

Saturday

Every day I see the world more clearly. Shadows become figures, white blurs become faces, dark holes become eyes with their desires and their problems. People you don't know and whom I hate because of that, but whom I must take note of and jot down in the margin of my life story— something I had hoped would never exist, only our joint life story and then the end. But here it is anyway, a sad and melancholy tale. I shake hands with some of the people here and ask how they are, and they in turn ask me how I am but hesitate to look at me. There are the young men at the beach, Mauro the moody one, and Mago and the engineer, two young people who share a room and work together on a construction project that makes the shore drive inaccessible just at the height of the summer season. There is a deep ditch, a high bank of earth, and a fiery-red machine that moves its ghostlike claws. In the evening these friends sit around at Cartuzza's and talk, that is, the engineer does the talking. After six years at the university, he knows how to string words together. But who would have paid poor Giulio, the one they call Mago, the rainmaker, to go to the university? He has had to work since he left high school. So he just sits there gazing at Costanza and looking away only when the boys jump off the terrace, which upsets him but leaves the engineer utterly cold. He doesn't even look. "Don't do that," pleads Mago. "You could land on a piece of glass down there or a rusty nail." But no one listens. The boys jump, and the engineer goes on talking, maybe about the grotto they discovered while they were working on the road (although only their boss's name was mentioned in the paper), or about the sea monster, the giant foot, and the large and small heads, this rock pile that didn't quite fit together, in which they were trying to see Laocoon encircled in snakes, but which they now think might be Polyphemus or Scylla, the sea monster. In the meantime it has gotten late. The music is playing, the engineer jumps up and, spoiled as he is, simply extends his hand toward Annamaria while Mago leans across the table toward Costanza and asks her to dance. And he smiles this indescribably sad smile so characteristic of southern Italian young men who are handsome and poor and hopelessly lonely.

Sunday

Some people always carry their chair or bed around with them like a snail does its house, only invisibly. Not until it actually materializes do we recognize the appropriateness of it and smile with relief. Yes, we think, that suits you, this office chair, this saddle, this wide bed, this coffin. For Annamaria the hammock was invented, but where do you ever come across a hammock these days? When we were children, we would lug hammocks, magnificently heavy bundles, with us to the pine forest where we would stretch them out across the narrow stream that rushed downhill between moss-covered stones. Intended for reading and sleeping but especially for daydreaming, they seemed to be part of our childhood so long ago and to be destined to perish with it. To my surprise we now have a hammock here too, even though it is a different kind of hammock. Woven of the thinnest nylon fibers, it can be stored in a small bag and needs no wooden hangers, so that it envelops the body of the person lying in it tightly like a fishnet, like a cocoon. The owner, who lent it to Annamaria, never uses it. He is one of these modern fellows, a restless and ambitious guy, for whom a day or simply a couple of hours of leisure is more than enough. But in our household the hammock has taken a place of honor. It is considered a rare and precious object that is greatly admired, and for lack of any other fancy treatment, we offer it to our guests as soon as they have arrived. They sit in it sideways, letting their feet dangle and pushing off against the tiles on the terrace so that they can swing in it. Costanza lies down in it once in a while with her work in her lap. But only Annamaria was born for the hammock; she alone carries it around with her invisibly, like the snail its house. She alone still knows how to dream those

75

old girlhood dreams, he and I, I and he, dreams that make it mandatory for him to have more than one face, one figure, one set of gestures. This face smiles at Annamaria, the old-fashioned girl, through the branches of the fig tree, and when she sways back and forth and casts her tender glances upward, I'm sure she also hears voices, many different voices all telling her the same thing. And this is actually the best part, for, needless to say, girls in hammocks are afraid of the reality of love and imagine it to be terrible. Their views of life hang in the balance: don't grab for it yet, don't latch on to anything yet, don't choose any of the numerous possibilities the future has in store because you will close the door to all others. Just sway back and forth in your net, in your cocoon, and smile tenderly at someone or no one at all. That's Annamaria, who is actually not my daughter at all but just thought to be that here. To describe her, all you can think of are words that are no longer in vogue: fickle, pert, coquettish, and she herself constructs an old child's world out of all diminutives: little house, little tree, little chicken. Relieving an old woman of her bundle of firewood whenever she gets a chance is as much a part of her as are the sudden fits of sadness and helplessness that cover her rosy-cheeked face with an expression of fear.

Monday

The interest I've started to take recently in people and things is already getting to me. I don't want to engage my imagination, don't want to invent things, don't want to feel pleasure so as to abandon you to your loneliness, your powerlessness, your silence which cannot speak. Instead of coming back with Costanza and Annamaria, who laugh and chatter all the time, I walk home from the beach alone under the pretext of needing something from the store or starting lunch. The road that I take by myself is a completely different one, hotter, brighter, and much longer. Although I have tied a black scarf underneath my big straw hat, the sun beats down mercilessly. There is not a soul around, no one comes toward me, and no one passes me. The houses sit there with closed shutters like empty seashells, a grille has been pulled across the door to the grocery store. My feet grind in the thick dust, I get gravel in my sandals, and I have to shake my feet to get rid of it. At a certain bend in the road a strong, sweet scent of citrus flowers wafts across a garden fence. I stop there for a moment, and I stop again by the uncultivated little plot full of dried-up artichoke plants, above whose wild iron spikes a few delicate blue flowers float as if they had fallen from heaven. Once in a while I run into the men whose job it is to spray the fields for insects, and somehow there is something pleasing about the looks of these totally foreign and non-human shapes with their elephant masks, their long-handled, white-spouted canisters, and their smocks dusted with greenish-blue powder. I am also pleased that at this hour no one talks, no one sings or turns on the radio, and that the only sound I hear is the insistent, irritating but totally inorganic chirping of countless crickets. When I take this road home, I almost don't think, not even of you. But it makes me feel good not to be seen by anyone and in a sense not to exist, because no one sees you anymore, and you no longer exist. My evenings alone (I take the girls over to Cartuzza's because that's the custom around here, la mamma, I have something to drink and walk back home)—my evenings are different, less inorganic, and more melancholy, plagued as they are by memories, frightened by apparitions.

Tuesday

By the light that falls on the terrace through the living room door, I read letters from the Great Beyond in a French book. A woman, whose son died at age fifteen, recorded daily over a period of years what her son said to her. The young angel is severe in the same way that all young sons are severe: his mother is too worldly for him, too distracted. He frequently found her unwilling to take an interest in him, even reluctant to encounter him. Because he died so young and so innocent, he is capable of establishing contact with her. He does not have to suffer any of the fires of purgatory, only a rather unspecified existence in the Beyond, and up until now the vision of the mother of God was denied him. The medium through which his voice becomes audible is their mutual faith—the bit of hokus pokus that accompanies also this spirit when he approaches (the rapping and the dancing lights in the dark) doesn't count. With love and impatience the son prepares his mother for heaven. She is to cut her ties with the earth, become his equal in spirit, all of which happens very fast in the paradise-like setting of the church. In her account, however, one waits in vain for an increase in spirituality, a lessening of worldliness, that would finally lead to a transcendent death. Nothing like that, but no defection either, no liberation from the superhuman discipline. The book is finished. But the dictation undoubtedly continues every night and sometimes even during the day, an act of will without equal, a loyalty beyond the grave, no matter whether the speaker is really her dead son or her own vivid imagination giving voice to a shadow. There must be a reason beside the theological one mentioned above that only a boy, who is practically still a child, can appear in this manner or be conjured up by his surviving mother. One cannot imagine someone older who has died (least of all you) to be so grimly humorless. One would sooner imagine such a person to have become exceedingly wise and tolerant at the point of passing over vis-à-vis the childish games that may still occupy the survivors here. In this regard, you see, I would not be afraid to establish contact with you. There is a completely different reason for my not taking pen to paper when I sit alone on the little terrace in the evenings totally occupied with thoughts of you. I could endure everything other than the fact that I might not hear anything, that I might not have anything to write down, and that just the shadows of the fig leaves would fall on the white paper, only to be gone by morning.

Wednesday

My old curiosity has been awakened again. For the first time since we arrived here, I have climbed up to the little town, a mountain village whose narrow streets and squares reverberate like machine shops from the clatter of engines. The pavement, which is divided into squares of black and white, imposes a pleasing order on whatever kinds of disorder have settled, litter of all sorts and little streams of dirty water. Here and there stairways with curving wrought-iron banisters lead up to the houses, and behind scrolled balcony railings roses and carnations bloom in old tin cans. Girls carry water home from the well in rounded jugs decorated with Mycenaean mollusks. On the house walls, announcements bordered in black mourn the death of a recent inhabitant, and on the stone bench by the town gate there are old people. Anyone entering or leaving the town must walk past them; it is like walking past markers that remind you that youth cannot last. The Templars are still present in the names of the streets and the inns, but the memory of the inhabitants is short, and the only past owner of the castle they can name is someone who acquired large sections of the mountain for a song two generations ago. The person who truly rules this place and probably always has is the ancient woman with the bony fingers and the ring of flies around her mouth. All skin and bones with fiery, crater-like eyes, she sits on the stone bench in front of her tiny house. An enormous hairy spider hovers above her head on the plastered wall behind her. If you peer through the half-drawn curtain into her windowless hovel, you see a bed full of gray rags and a stove, above which hang bundles of dried herbs. There is no way of talking to the old woman. Not that she is deaf or dumb; she is just completely indifferent, her mind on something that is hidden to us, something that has been going on for thousands of years. Since you come across her again and again not just here in the country but in the cities as well not a hundred yards from the gleaming marble façades, and since she is present not just once but again and again, I am quite familiar with her and know her other faces as well, some of them frightening, as if she were capable of wandering around at night and strangling little children in their sleep. I have a sense of her toughness, the toughness of ants, which the heaviest foot cannot eradicate. I also have a sense of her ruthlessness and her complicity with illness and hopelessness and despair. Efforts to get rid of her are underway, and her old dilapidated shack was torn down behind her back. Then she probably got up without a word and moved on, only to find another place to sit down again, in front of a Quonset hut or a cave on the slope of the mountain, or in one of the cheap suburban high-rises, whose steep, cliff-like walls admit no light. There she sits then, the way I saw her in the mountain village today, motionless, with a ring of flies around her bluish lips and an old triumph in her bloodshot eyes. But the spider above her head has finished its web and is lying in wait in the noonday sun, a pitch-black dot on a dazzling white wall.

Thursday

Wandering around alone—with you, that is, as we did before, only without talking or getting answers, without touching, without nods of agreement—on Circe's mountain, which has flat swampy land around its base. This mountain belongs to the Mediterranean islands, not to the mainland. The people who live up there are really islanders, and it is not hard to imagine all the possible acts of violence that take place on these secluded islands: vendettas, sibling revenge, taking justice into one's own hands. Today I saw several men standing in a grape arbor and putting their heads together. They pointed to a man in city clothes, who had apparently arrived by bus and was now walking up the steep mountain road. He was not a stranger but one of them, and yet they seemed to have something against him and to be plotting to play a trick on him or do something even worse. The man didn't notice them. Like someone returning after a long absence, he walked with his head thrust back and looked straight ahead at the houses that lay clustered below the summit. With a happy smile on his face he seemed to fix his gaze on one particular one. I felt like warning him, but that was just because of a story I had heard that had taken place somewhere else, on a real island. What happened here had nothing to do with that and might be quite harmless. In the story nothing was harmless. The man who came back was a Cypriote who had collaborated with the British and who had remained with them until right after the end of the hostilities, thus enjoying their protection from his own countrymen. He had spent several months in a military compound surrounded by barbed wire; he was well fed, and he was treated humanely. But as time went by, he got so homesick for his mountain village that he became physically ill and finally asked permission to go home. The British sent along an officer who accompanied him to the entrance to his village but was then only too happy to leave him to his own devices. In the meantime the returning man was already being watched as he came up the mountain, and the news of his arrival had spread. The townspeople had assembled in front of his house as if to welcome him, but what occurred was not a celebration but a sentencing. The man's wife had sensed something was wrong. She had been about to run out to warn her husband, but they tied her to the bedpost with ropes, leaving the door to the room open. She was not to witness what would happen to her husband; wives of traitors were not innocent. Hanging in her ropes, she cried and hollered as she watched her relatives and old friends drag out gasoline cans and bundles of straw. You see, they planned to dowse the homesick traitor with gasoline and then set fire to him like a torch, and that's exactly what they did. The man was much too surprised to protest, or perhaps he didn't expect anything else but felt compelled to return home anyway. It was this horrible scene that came to mind today as I stood there by the grape arbor listening for sounds from the place up there where all the men from the grape arbor and the returning man as well had disappeared, albeit via different roads. But there were no screams to be heard, nothing at all terrible, only the distant cheerful sound of a brass band striking up a welcome march.

Friday

I should think sitting in a motorboat that rises halfway out of the water while performing the most daring leaps and turns across the waves at high speed would give one a feeling of the supernatural. As I hung on to the rim of the boat, my face was covered with spray, salt, and wind. I did experience this feeling of freedom which we call divine when I was invited for a ride today, but at the same time the most violent and unpleasant jolts shook my body again and again as the boat hit the water. The motor made an earsplitting noise, and my view of the beach kept changing: now the white sand with the colorful umbrellas, now the ragged rocky coast, and already we were heading south again toward Terracina and the Temple of Jupiter. The speed transformed the boat into a mythical bird, the rough bumps made it seem more like a wild mustang whose bucking so disorients the rider that he can hardly stay on. But then the motor stalled, and for a while we floated silently across the water, and everything was suddenly as it should be again: a clear head, the algae forests, the fishes, and Vineta deep below the water's surface, raising its shadowy towers and ringing its mysterious bells. I remembered coming back from a boat trip in the evening from a more southerly beach and bending over the water. There were real ruins there, the remains of a city gradually covered with water, but even then I thought what was really down there at the bottom was the great landscape of the dead and not just those who had drowned. Eventually everything that had lived and loved and suffered on earth would end up there, and all memories as well. Most likely the same places would continue to exist on land and below, only down below they embodied their past, a time that could not be relived. For me, that was where Rome, Athens, and Istanbul were today, these cities we had enjoyed together. These submerged cities were the real ones, and there was nothing funereal about them. All I would have to do, I thought, was just slip down there to be surrounded once more by the exuberant life they once held for you and me. While the boat still drifted along soundlessly, I thought of Vineta as a great bazaar of memories, of the conversations that resound from there and of the forgotten faces that look out the windows. I didn't pay any attention to the owner of the boat, who cursed as he started to fix the motor. I heard only the voice of my young companion who cheerfully offered to pick a bouquet of algae, "for you, Madame," as he started to dive into the deep. But then, as the motor sputtered violently, we were suddenly catapulted forward again. The beach whizzed past, the rocks and the lighthouse. The ocean closed and became a surface hard as glass on which we executed our unruly dance. Everything—the heat of the sun, the flying spray, and the naked deep blue sky—screamed again its relentless "today, today."

Saturday

To go away and come back, to remove yourself from the world and other people and then come back to them again is a movement of uneven strokes of the pendulum, short periods, long periods of eclipse or of light.

The darkness of seclusion demands that you bring the lessons learned from this darkness back with you. You can't just pick up where you left off and go on as before. This is even more true after a journey to the limits of the bearable, a half death. New words, you would think, would have to offer themselves to the writer and new colors to the painter, and the thinker would have to express connections he had never grasped before. Unfortunately this is not the case. Even after the most excruciating experience, you obey the laws of gravity: your legs are down and your head is up. You wake up, get dressed, and go out, while remaining firmly within the skin you had wanted to shed, at least in a manner of speaking. You have become sadder and probably less curious, but not new, and you have no more words at your disposal than before to express the unheard-of. Your intonation, too, is the same; without some wrenching spasm it does not change. You are not just a part of yourself but also a part of your generation. Even major heart-rending experiences do not result in the discovery of the language of tomorrow. The language of today is really of no use to the older writer, who leaves room for reality and sensual perception, and for whom the symbol still has not completely replaced the image. Not to want to continue as before is the wish of everyone who has not chosen his new beginning but has had it imposed on him without knowing for what purpose and to what end. At least this much you want: to jump off the old track, to find ways of escape, to reappear with a new voice and a new face. Instead you are still the same old person. Even now you have little more to say than before, and you have not discovered any new forms. Once in a while it may even seem to you as if the years spent in darkness have magically multiplied so that you no longer understand the language spoken around you and the importance of the things other people consider important. The only thing left to you, then, other than to remain silent, is monologue, monologue conducted with discipline and hard work. That may still have some meaning because of this very discipline and hard work—an accountability to yourself as you continue to write the way you didn't want to and with a heavier heart than before.

Sunday

To continue to write, to continue to live, with a heavier heart than before. Our suitcases are packed; we have spent our last night by Circe's Mountain; the last dance music has sounded across the dark beach: "Catch a Falling Star," "Hang down your Head and Cry," a ball trying to get through the clanging obstacle course to its dark place of safety and being knocked back again, numbers lighting up like magic, whoever can hold on the longest, wins. I don't want to hold on any longer, I don't want to be knocked back and forth between these gaudy markers. Yet something has driven me back into life and opened my eyes: so far you have managed to avoid the hole, do make an effort. It's up to you to make something of it. Each day I have seen and heard and thought a little more without forgetting my loved one. He was always there, in fact so much so that I'm almost afraid he will stay behind here when I get on the bus, San Felice-Roma, there in front of the Hotel Neanderthal where they keep that prehistoric skull in a cave. They will all be there waving: the dissimilar young men and the dissimilar sisters and the hairdresser and the photographer with his funny little African cap. He had taken pictures of Costanza, once as a flower among flowers in a garden and another time in her bathing suit, with a frightened question mark in her eyes although that was not his intent. The same old dance tunes and voices come from Majolatis's beach terrace; after all, it's just July, the summer season is still going strong. The autumn storms, the early evenings, the many lonely hours of September are still far away. Our cottage has been rented out again. As I write this, the new family is already standing in front of the terrace, and Annamaria wants to put the little dark-haired boys in the hammock before she takes it down and folds it up. But the children are afraid, for they have never seen anything like that before. Taking leave of the fig tree is the hardest. Its fruits are ripe now, but dry, almost inedible. It was my companion on the terrace at night, an enchanted human being who sometimes sighed and moved his arms. But it was not you. You are not banned into one form, and I am homeless and restless because I don't know where to find you. I fear you might remain behind here. I already picture us leaving. The road winds around twice and runs along the back of the mountain, the head of Circe, thrust back and turned to stone. The grounds of the Roman villa, already divided into lots, are still a wilderness. As we drive away, your airy steps are perhaps already speeding toward the hall of the enchantress, toward the dark shrubs from which Odysseus saw mysterious puffs of smoke rise and wolves and mountain lions rushed to greet him.

The Fat Girl

It was at the end of January, shortly after the Christmas break, that the fat girl showed up. I had started lending out books to the children in our neighborhood that winter, which they were supposed to pick up and return on a certain day every week. I knew most of these children, of course, but occasionally there were some I didn't know, some who didn't live in our neighborhood. Although most of them stayed around only long enough to exchange their books, there were always others who would sit down and start reading right away. When that happened, I would sit at my desk and write, and the children would be at the little table by the bookshelves. Their presence was enjoyable and didn't bother me at all.

The fat girl showed up on a Friday or Saturday, in any case not on the day agreed upon for the exchange. I was planning to go out and was just about to carry the little lunch I had fixed into the living room. Just before that I had had a visitor, and my guest had probably neglected to close the front door. That would explain how the fat girl happened to be standing in front of me so suddenly, just as I was putting down my tray on the desk and turning around to go get something else from the kitchen. She was about twelve years old and wore an old-fashioned loden coat and black, knitted spats, and she carried a pair of skates on a strap. She seemed familiar and yet unfamiliar, and because she had slipped in so quietly, she startled me.

"Do I know you?" I asked surprised.

The fat girl didn't answer. She just stood there with her hands across her fat stomach, looking at me with eyes that were clear as water.

"Would you like a book?" I asked.

The fat girl still didn't answer, but I didn't give it much thought. I was used to children being shy and needing help. So I pulled out a couple of books and placed them in front of the strange girl. Then I began to fill out one of the cards on which I recorded the checked-out books.

"So what's your name?" I asked.

"They call me 'fatso'," the girl said.

"Is that what you want me to call you?" I asked.

"I don't care," the girl said. She didn't return my smile, and I seem to recall that she winced just then. But I didn't pay much attention.

"When were you born?" I continued.

"In Aquarius," the girl said calmly.

Since this answer amused me, I wrote it down on the card, for the fun of it as it were, and then I turned back to the books again.

"Is there anything special you would like?" I asked.

But then I noticed that the strange girl wasn't looking at the books at all but had her eyes fixed on the tray with my tea and sandwiches instead.

"Maybe you would like something to eat?" I said quickly.

The girl nodded, and there was something about the expression on her face that suggested a kind of wounded surprise at the fact that I hadn't thought about that before. She started to devour one sandwich after another, and she did so in a special way, which I didn't think to account for until later. Then she sat there again and let her cold, listless eyes roam around the room, and there was something about her that filled me with anger and loathing. Frankly, I hated this girl from the very beginning. I found everything about her repulsive: her lethargic movements, her pretty, fat face, her way of speaking, which had something drowsy and pushy about it at the same time. And although I had decided to forget about my walk for her sake, I can't say I treated her very nicely. If anything, I was cruel and cold.

It was certainly not very nice of me to go over to my desk and sit down and work while saying over my shoulder: "Go on, read," when I knew perfectly well that the strange girl couldn't care less about reading. I sat there trying to write but couldn't because I felt strangely bothered, as if I were supposed to guess something and couldn't, and until I had guessed it, nothing would ever be the way it was before. I could take it for a while, but only for so long; then I turned around and struck up a conversation with her, although I could think of only the most banal things to say.

"Do you have any brothers or sisters?" I asked.

"Sure," the girl said.

"Do you like school?" I asked.

"Sure," said the girl.

"What do you like best?"

"What do you mean?" the girl asked.

"What subject?" I said desperately.

"I don't know," the girl said.

"Maybe German?" I asked.

"I don't know," said the girl.

I rolled the pencil between my fingers, and something welled up in me, a fear that had nothing to do with the fact that the girl had shown up.

"Do you have any girlfriends?" I asked in a trembly voice.

"Oh, sure," said the girl.

"I bet there's one you like better than the rest?" I asked.

"I don't know," the girl said, and as she sat there in her hairy loden coat, she looked like a fat caterpillar. Come to think of it, she had also eaten like a fat caterpillar, and now she was sniffing around like a caterpillar as well.

Now you're not getting any more, I thought, filled with a strange desire for revenge, but then I went out and got some bread and luncheon meat after all. The girl stared at it impassively; then she began to eat, the way a caterpillar eats, slowly and persistently, as if out of some inner compulsion, and I watched her with silent hostility.

Because now things had gotten to the point when everything about this girl was starting to irritate and upset me. What a silly-looking white dress, what a ridiculous-looking stand-up collar, I thought, when the girl unbuttoned her coat after she had eaten. I began to write again, but then I heard the girl smack her lips behind me, and this sound was like the sluggish lapping of a black pond in the woods somewhere. It made me acutely aware of everything murky, everything painful and sad about human nature, and it made me utterly depressed. What do you want from me? I thought. Go away. Get out of here. I felt like pushing the girl out of the room with my own hands, the way you shoo away a pesky animal. But then I didn't push her out of the room after all; instead I just kept talking to her in the same cruel way.

"Are you going skating now?" I asked.

"Yep," said the fat girl.

"Are you any good at it?" I asked, pointing to the skates that were still dangling from the girl's arm.

"My sister is," said the girl. Once more she had an expression of sadness and pain on her face, and again I ignored it.

"What does your sister look like?" I asked. "Does she look like you?"

"Oh, no," said the fat girl. "My sister is quite thin and has curly black hair. In the summertime when we're in the country, she gets up at night when there's a thunderstorm and sits on the banister all the way up on the top landing and sings."

"And you?" I asked.

"I stay in bed," said the girl. "I'm scared."

"Your sister isn't scared then?" I said.

"No," said the girl. "She's never scared. She dives from the highest diving board. She jumps right in, and then she swims way out ..."

"What does your sister sing?" I asked curiously.

"Whatever she wants to," the fat girl said sadly. "She makes up poems."

"And you?" I asked.

"I don't do anything," the girl said. Then she got up and said she had to leave. I held out my hand, and she put her chubby fingers in it. I don't quite know what I felt when she did that, something like a plea to follow her, an inaudible, urgent call.

"Stop by again some time," I said, but I didn't mean it, and the girl didn't say anything either; she just looked at me with her impassive gaze, then she was gone. I guess I should have felt relieved, but I had scarcely heard the front door bang shut before I ran out in the hall and put on my coat. I raced down the stairs and reached the street just as the girl was disappearing around the next corner.

I've simply got to see how this caterpillar does on skates, I thought. I've simply got to see how this lump of fat moves on the ice. And I quickened my pace so as not to lose sight of the girl.

It had been early afternoon when the fat girl showed up in my room, and now it was starting to get dark. Although I had spent a few years in this town as a child, I didn't know my way around that well anymore, and while I tried hard to follow the girl, it wasn't long before I had no idea which way we were going; the streets and squares that I passed were totally unfamiliar. I also suddenly became aware of a change in the weather. It had been very cold, but now a thaw must have set in, and with such intensity that the snow was already dripping from the roofs and big storm clouds were drifting across the sky. We reached the outskirts of town where the houses are surrounded by large gardens. Then there were no houses anymore, and the girl suddenly disappeared down a slope. But whereas I had expected to see a skating rink with lighted booths and arc lamps and a shimmering surface with happy voices and all kinds of music, I now saw an entirely different scene. For down there was the lake whose shores I had thought were completely built up by now: it lay there all by itself surrounded by dark woods, and it looked exactly the way it had when I was a child.

This unexpected scene upset me so that I almost lost sight of the strange girl. But then I saw her again. She was sitting by the shore trying to put one leg over the other and to fasten the skate to her boot with one hand while turning the key with the other. She dropped the key a couple of times, and then she got down on her hands and knees and slid around on the ice searching for it, all the while looking like a strange toad. In the meantime it was getting darker. The pier, which jutted out into the lake just a few feet away from the girl, loomed pitch-black above the wide surface which glistened silvery, not all over but a bit darker here and there, and in those opaque areas the thaw made itself known. "Hurry up," I shouted impatiently, and the fat girl actually did hurry up now, not at my urging but because out there, right at the end of the long pier, someone was waving and calling: "Come on, fatso"—someone who was tracing circles, a light, bright figure. I realized this had to be her sister, the dancer, the one who would sing during a thunderstorm, a girl after my own heart, and I was suddenly convinced that the only thing that had lured me out here was the desire to see this graceful person. At the same time, however, I also became aware of the danger the children were in. For now this strange moaning suddenly started, these deep sighs that the lake seems to utter before the ice cover breaks. These sighs reverberated in the depths like a terrible lament, and I heard it, but the children didn't.

No, I'm sure they didn't hear it. Because otherwise the fat girl, that little coward, wouldn't have started out; she wouldn't have ventured farther out with her scraping clumsy thrusts; and her sister out there wouldn't have waved and laughed and pirouetted like a ballerina only to trace her beautiful figure eights again; and the fat girl would have avoided the black patches, which she was now trying to stay clear of only to scramble across them again; and her sister wouldn't suddenly have stood up straight and skated off, away, away, toward one of the little isolated coves.

I was able to observe all this in some detail because I had started to wander out on the pier, farther and farther, step by step. Although the planks were ice-covered, I nevertheless moved more quickly than the fat girl down below, and when I turned around, I could see her face, which had an expression of both indifference and longing. I could also see the cracks that were opening up everywhere, out of which foamy water appeared like the foam around the lips of a madman. And then, of course, I saw the ice giving way underneath the fat girl. For that occurred on the very spot where her sister had just danced and only a few arms lengths from the end of the pier.

I want to make the point right here that this breaking up of the ice was not anything life threatening. The lake freezes in a couple of layers, and the second one was only a few feet below the first and still quite solid. The only thing that happened was that the fat girl was standing in three feet of water, and in icy water at that, surrounded by cracking ice floes, but if she would take just a few steps through the water, she could reach the pier and pull herself up, and I would be there to lend a helping hand. But my first thought was still that she wouldn't make it, and it certainly didn't look as if she would, the way she stood there frightened to death and making just a few awkward movements while the water swirled around her and the ice broke beneath her hands. Aquarius, I thought, now he is pulling her down. I didn't even feel anything when I had that thought, not the slightest pity for her. And I didn't move.

But now the fat girl suddenly raised her head, and because night had finally arrived and the moon had appeared from behind the clouds, I could clearly see that something in her face had changed. Her features were the same and yet not the same. They were imbued with will and passion as if now, in the face of death, they were drinking in all life, all the glowing life in the world. Indeed, I was thoroughly convinced that death was near and that this was the end. I peered over the railing and looked into the white face below me, and like my own reflection it looked back at me from the black water. But by now the fat girl had reached the post. She had reached out and started to pull herself up; she held on quite deftly to the nails and hooks that projected from the wood. Her body was too heavy, her fingers were bleeding, and she kept falling back in, but she would start over again. It was a long struggle I was witnessing, a terrible struggle for deliverance and transformation, like the breaking up of a shell or a cocoon. At this point I should have helped the girl, I guess, but I knew she no longer needed my help—I had recognized her ...

I have no recollection of how I got home that evening. I only know that when I ran into a neighbor of mine on the stairs I told her there was still a stretch of lake shore left with meadows and dark woods, but she said there was no such thing. Later that night I found among the disorderly piles of paper on my desk an old photograph of myself in a white wool dress with a stand-up collar—with bright watery eyes and so very fat.

A Noon Hour in Mid-June

I was just coming back from a trip and hadn't heard a thing. I came straight home from the train station and rang the doorbell at my neighbor's where I had left my keys. She was very happy to see me and made a face fraught with meaning.

"Did you know you were dead?" she asked.

Although I never thought life was that great, her words had a strange effect on me.

"What do you mean 'dead'?" I asked.

"Come now," said my neighbor (her name is Frau Teichmann) "don't take it too hard. Whoever is pronounced dead has a long life."

I forced myself to smile and took my keys, which she had put away in her desk drawer.

"Who told you I was dead?" I asked.

"A stranger," Frau Teichmann said. "Nobody knew her. She came into the building and started ringing everybody's doorbell and telling everyone you were dead. She had dark-brown skin and an emaciated face. I'm sure she was from some foreign country."

"From Italy?" I asked.

But Frau Teichmann didn't know about that. She seemed to recall that the stranger had had a magazine in her hand. Maybe the woman had been trying to sell magazine subscriptions in the buildings, but my neighbor didn't remember the name of the magazine.

"There're so many people coming around these days," she said. "Young men, too. Yesterday someone was at the door, and all he could say was: 'Christ is here!'" Then she went on to tell how the strange woman had asked for the keys to my apartment, had in fact demanded that they be handed over to her right then and there.

"That's really disgusting," I said upset. I thanked her and went over to my apartment, where I unpacked and looked through the pile of third-class mail that had not been forwarded. I tried not to think about the strange incident anymore, but I had no luck. You invariably feel at loose ends whenever you get home, in any case especially when you're not used to being alone. Objects greet you differently from people. What they demand of you is at least to be dusted off, and then they immediately shower you with memories of all sorts. You walk around and tend to this, that, and the other. After all, it was not always that quiet here, and then you sit

90

down and close your eyes because you simply can't look around anymore without it hurting. So I sat down, and no sooner had I closed my eyes than I thought about the strange woman again and about how nice it would be to know more about her, the most minute thing, the most minuscule detail.

It was five o'clock now, and frankly I would have liked to fix myself a cup of tea. But instead I went down to see Frau Hoesslin, the woman who lives below me, and after that I went to check with the family that lives upstairs. I did learn a thing or two, but not a whole lot, and when I got back to my own place again, I tried to imagine how it had been that noon hour in mid-June. That was two months ago now. Noon and mid-June and hot, all the women on the stairs, summoned by the loud foreign-sounding voice, and Herr Frohwein, a traveling salesman, on his way out the door, and on a landing somewhere the impostor showing up completely self-assured and downright aggressive. "Believe me," she said, "Frau Kaschnitz is no longer alive. She's dead as sure as I'm standing here." The women shake their heads, and Herr Frohwein instinctively removes his hat. All of them are taken aback but not quite convinced. Since we have been living in this large apartment building for a long time, all the tenants know me fairly well. In fact, we used to spend entire nights in the air raid shelter together, not to mention getting down on the floor with them whenever the bombs were falling nearby. Frau Hoesslin had forwarded my mail, and I had sometimes shown my gratitude for this by sending her postcards of the Roman fountains or of the coast at Cape Circe. In fact, a postcard like that, from Cape Circe, had arrived just a few days ago. I had written I was fine, and my daughter had added a line. My death, therefore, seemed improbable but, of course, not impossible. After all, there are such things as storms and undertows and sharks; accidents and heart attacks do occur; and how many people don't leave this world of their own free will? In other words, there was reason enough to shake your head suspiciously, but not reason enough to hand over the key, especially to a total stranger.

"As sure as you're standing here!" Frau Teichmann says. "That's all very well, but just who is standing here? We don't know you from Adam. We never laid eyes on you before."

"My name isn't going to change anything," the woman says quickly. "I've been authorized. That ought to be good enough."

"And why you of all persons?" Frau Teichmann starts again.

"Because Frau Kaschnitz was all alone," the stranger says, with a toss of her head, "because she had no one else in the world."

Now the women get all fired up, and everyone starts talking at once.

"Didn't have anyone? That's not true. That's ridiculous. She had visitors, almost every day, friends or relatives, and her phone rang all the time, and her mailbox was always crammed full."

They utter all this with great conviction, and it's a wonder the strange woman isn't intimidated by it. She stands quite erect on the stairs and shouts loudly that it isn't so. "I know better. She had no one. She was all alone in the world."

This was as far as I got with my reenactment of the scene. The story wasn't quite finished yet, but after the last sentence I was stuck. It kept going around in my head, and to get rid of it I walked around my apartment looking out the windows to this side and that. Down on the street a policeman was holding a little girl by the hand. In cases like this, I thought, you've got to notify the police, and I don't really see why they didn't do that right away. Or did they? No, they didn't. Herr Teichmann had merely mumbled something about the police to his wife, and thereupon, or not at all thereupon, the stranger had stuck the magazine back in her briefcase and taken off, but not at all as if she were trying to escape. Extremely slowly, like a slighted monarch, she descended the stairs without deigning to speak to anyone.

I've got to find the woman with the magazines, I thought. People who go around selling magazines must be on the streets or in the buildings around here, and why shouldn't she be back in this neighborhood again? So I put on my gloves; I didn't need a jacket since it was still warm outside, a summer without end. I went down to the street and waited around at the different entrances to the buildings and in front of the doors, and then I tried the side streets. I also asked about the stranger in the stores that were still open. But no one had seen her, not that other time either, and of all the solicitors only a scissors grinder was still around and a man who was driving his tarpaulin-covered apple cart home. In fact, it was getting dark now; the days were already shorter, the nights longer, a fact which even the hottest of suns cannot conceal. On my way home, I went by way of the police station, but they had relocated in the meantime, and I was suddenly very tired and didn't feel like taking another step. I also imagined how aggravating it would be for the people in my building to be questioned, probably even blamed. They would have to come up with answers, and they were likely to be caught in contradictions. Was the woman wearing a hat? Yes, no, of course not, or maybe she was after all. Finally they themselves would look like common criminals although they had acted quite sensibly and refused to give out the key. In any case, they obviously didn't want to have anything to do with the police since they hadn't called at the time. The woman had been so weird. She might come back and retaliate, maybe leave a bunch of oakum on the basement steps and set a match to it, which would be child's play since our house door unfortunately is always open.

So I didn't go to the police station after all but went home instead, and there I had this idea. I got out my notebook, which is actually a calendar but the kind that has lots of room for writing next to every date. Suddenly it was of the utmost importance to me to find out what had happened to me on that day in mid-June, but why it was so important I didn't know.

Friday the thirteenth, Saturday the fourteenth, Sunday the fifteenth of June. It wasn't clear exactly on what date the stranger had entered the building. It would really be asking too much of my neighbors to get them to remember that as well. A day around noon in mid-June, that's what they had all said, and that meant it couldn't be a Friday because Frau Hoesslin was in the Taunus at that time, and it couldn't be a Saturday either because Herr Frohwein didn't work on Saturdays, and on Sunday no one would be selling magazines. On Monday the woman above me had her cleaning lady in, and she would have been sure to be out on the stairs, nosy as she is. In other words, it came down to the seventeenth or the eighteenth of June. I went ahead and checked my calendar for the seventeenth and the eighteenth. I didn't do this just standing over my half-unpacked suitcase but sat down at my desk after having pulled the drapes and turned on the floor lamp, everything very solemnly as if I were about to make God only knows what kind of a discovery. But there was absolutely nothing recorded for the eighteenth and very little for the seventeenth; actually only the words "drink," "drown," and "Orpheus," and those words didn't make any sense.

I've often wondered why we'll write down certain things only if they can be written in code or disguised somehow or other, things we might blurt out later on but which at this particular moment are not yet transformed and, therefore, still fraught with danger. I thought about that, too, now: dangerous, danger, caution flag, a little piece of red cloth waving on a bamboo pole above the beach. Storm, undertow, danger, no swimming. But that's not the way it was at all that noon in mid-June. Suddenly I remembered exactly how it was: deep-blue sky, the familiar reflection of the ocean, its tiny almost inaudible waves brushing the shore, a scorching sun, the sand glowing hot. The hour of panic and terror in southern climes, and I myself swimming out, all alone as it were. On the white sand under the umbrella are my black clothes, black hose, black shoes. Costanza and her girlfriend and Mago and the engineer had gone for a drink; the bar is a couple of steps higher up facing away from the sea; the jukebox next to the dance floor is blaring and wailing and then silent. The English children are called to lunch; whoever else is around squints into the sun without stirring. The water along this coast is very shallow. I'm far away from the shore before I can really swim; I can no longer make out the faces and the figures. I turn on my back; the heavy salt water buoys me; I need not move a muscle; I clasp my hands behind my head. The houses are tiny: above them the forests rise, and above them the cliffs, the head of Circe twisted backward with pain and turned to stone. Poor enchantress, I think. You who didn't know how to do anything, who couldn't hold on to Odysseus even with all your magic cunning; whoever wants to leave, leaves, even if you promise him eternal love; whoever must roam, roams; and whoever must die, dies. Then I stop thinking and just swim farther out, keeping my eyes open under the water and seeing way down below me the pattern of waves in the fine sand. To raise my head above water is terrible, a feeling of loneliness beyond compare. I ought to swim back, get dressed, go to lunch. But why should I? It's all in vain anyway; I couldn't hold on to you, Odysseus; you had to go away to fulfill your destiny, away to Ithaca, and Ithaca is death. I'm not an enchantress, not an immortal; I need not be turned to stone and stand against the sky like some awesome monument. I can drink, drown, sink down into the deep, rise to the surface; above and below it's all the same, above and below there are the blessed spirits, above and below there is you. An accident, a heart attack; no one needs to blame himself. Drink, drown, and the water is already foaming and roaring, grayish-white, greenish-white whirlpools pushing against my chest. A little deeper; it squeezes my chest, it constricts my throat. But where does that sound come from, the sound of a flute? Costanza never brings her flute along when she goes swimming; the sand would ruin it. Besides, you wouldn't be able to hear her play this far from the beach. But I do hear it, this sound of a flute without any hint of pastoral poetry about it. Instead it has a completely new sound, a strong and wild sound. By no means do I think now—insofar as it is possible to think in a few seconds—by no means do I think that Costanza is there now, that life is not pointless, that I'm not alone in the world. Because that much I do know: children are children and have their own lives. You can enjoy them and get angry at them and worry about them, but they can't help you. Yet it is this mysterious sound of the flute, this call to life, that pulls me up to the surface and keeps me above water, gasping, coughing, spitting. I lie on my back and rest, and I finally make my first arm movements toward the shore. On the shore Costanza is actually waiting with the towel in her hand and saying angrily, "Just what do you think you're doing, swimming out that far? Don't you know there're sharks out there?" We pack up our belongings, and I tell her not to forget her flute, and she looks at me bewildered. That was at twenty after twelve; by that time the strange woman had already left the apartment building back home. Why, I wonder? Surely not because she was afraid of the police?

I still had to find out why. Stiff-legged and half blind I got up from my desk, staggered out, and rang my neighbor's doorbell. She had already gone to bed, so she merely opened the little window in her front door.

"Excuse me," I said through the window. "I didn't quite understand why the woman who said I was dead finally did leave, and I really would like to know."

"But surely you aren't still thinking about that?" my neighbor said. "I told you whoever is pronounced dead has a long life."

"I would still like to know," I said.

"Oh, didn't I tell you?" said Frau Teichmann kindly. "Someone mentioned your daughter. Then the woman gave up and left."

Frau Teichmann shivered and yawned. It was almost eleven o'clock.

"Did you notify the police?" she asked.

But I hadn't, of course, nor did I intend to.

Walks

Talk, walk; silence, walk; ask, walk; answer, walk; point, smile as you shout "watch out," walk; say "you know," say "tomorrow," or "I'm tired, I can't walk another step." Roads, paths taken together, the last pedestrians, a couple in the street, a couple of demons. One time we walked through an unreal landscape on a narrow strip of sand between water and water, salt water and fresh water, inlet and ocean. There was sand beneath our feet, white dune sand, shifting and drifting from the salt water side toward the fresh water side, drifting through the houses, completely devouring them. Many decades later, they reappear at the back of the wave of dunes, gnawed away at, bleached like fish skeletons, and utterly silent. Between water and water we walked through forests that we could see out over as the trees bent and swayed in the sweeping winds. In the distance, mythical beasts with palmed antlers crossed the aisle, heavy torsos with a light, springy gait. We sat in one of these skeleton houses, making patterns out of blue shells, cross and star. Sand is like time; it, too, drifts through us, finally leaving us behind like a pile of bare bones. But we didn't give much thought to things like that then. We got up and walked on, and above our heads the migratory birds screeched.

Another time we climbed down to the coast from a mountain village in the South, and night was almost upon us. The sun was still there, just a flame flickering on the highest slope and then going out. The road, narrow and precipitous, was paved with flat stones. To the right and to the left lay the paper mills, darkish buildings from which mysterious noises could be heard, like roaring and pounding. In the paneless windows bundles of rags hung like bats as did childrens' faces, serious and pale. Farther down, the valley became wider and friendlier, grapes were harvested and nuts beaten off the trees. The village that we entered was a maze of white-plastered steps and covered walkways with front doors and house numbers, windows full of red geraniums, and black cats munching away on fish heads. Somewhere along the way a door opened. In glass shrines stood saints made of wax, lifeless and frightening, and out of crumpled beds crawled beautiful, pale children, more and more of them, like larvae out of a swamp. Outside, the bell hammered away. We walked on, and when we got to the beach, it was dark, and the first fishermen lit their lamps and rowed out on the ocean.

In the area where I come from we walked around the Mount of Olives, the great scenic route along the glacial stream, but this was no promenade, dry and comfortable. In the beech forest the path led upward toward the vineyards, then continued through barren grapevines. Heavy yellow clay stuck to our shoes, and we sometimes had to scratch it off with little sticks. Around the mountain there was a road with deep ruts in it, whose puddles reflected the blue sky. It was Christmas time, but what did that mean around here? Not snow by any means but periods when violets bloomed, periods when the föhn roared, with wonderful sunny days in between. On a Sunday like that we walked around the summit of the mountain, past primeval caves and rings to which boats were once fastened during an age when the ocean still hit the chalky rocks. We sat at the forest edge, near arching hedge roses and the gray wool of wild clematis, holding the thorny branches away from each other's face. I saw mostly the drifting clouds, the white star flowers, the reddish grapevines tied with yellow bast against the deep blue sky, the stream shimmering here and there on the plain below, everything that had always existed and always would. You saw mostly the Chemin des Dames, the Burgundian Gate, the Vosges Mountains, the Jura, the arenas of historical migrations and warlike conflicts, everything that had had its time, its past, that would never return. What we saw, we shared with one another. We continued our walk, and between flaming mackerel clouds the great gentle wind of the Rhine valley drove the sun to its glorious setting before our eyes.

Before the gates of Rome we descended the stairs to the underground chambers. It smelled of must and darkness, and in the light of your candle, signs of the cross and of fishes emerged from the walls next to marble sarcophagi. A draft of air blew out our only light, and for the longest time we could not find our way out of this labyrinth in the deep, from which no call could be heard above. When we finally saw daylight again, we embraced the white glowing sun and the earth, which abounded with wheat and wine. Then we continued our walk along the Appian Way, which became more isolated, a lane now, then a footpath among chamomile, daisies, and wild red poppies, toward the mountains, the village of Albano. The crickets chirped. The rosy evening light shone in the arches of the aqueduct, and a shepherd carried a newborn lamb, fleecy and bloody, on his shoulders toward the flock. We took this road hundreds of times later on. It changed with the times. Suddenly a layer of asphalt covered the old Roman stones, and the glistening string of lights that moved on it no longer let up at night. We couldn't walk anymore but had to drive instead: quo vadis, domine, Caecilia Metella—over and done with in a hurry; and almost just as fast the millipedes from the glistening suburbs staggered toward the mountains. In the old taverns, reserved wealthy patrons were served by countless waiters in white uniforms, and with a frightening roar angry planes came crashing through the sky as they landed at the airport. Even so, nothing was lost. The crickets still chirped and became silent in the evening, and the rosy glow remained in the arches of the aqueduct.

Mushroom patches form serpentine lines, zigzag lines; find them, check them out. With hopes dashed, run a little farther or go back where you came from. The forest is unreal with its streaks of mist, its wilderness of touch-me-nots, its tree trunks covered with ivy, like the props in a theater: only the white cap, the sand-brown tuber, the gray umbrella, the yellow coral is real. Shouts, whistle calls pass from one person to the other; our bent backs are already lost in the autumn mist and the approaching night. One time we hunted for mushrooms on a forest floor in Hessen. A plane approached fast and low, a machine gun clattered; we threw ourselves on the ground right where we were, our faces in the blackberries and up again, covered with blood and bluish-red juice. The little sack with the mushrooms we had just gathered was lost, and we searched for it as if for the Holy Grail. We sadly continued our walk through the darkening forest as if everything had depended on this evening meal, and as if our future life and love had been called into question. All the mushrooms had crept back into the earth; in the village the all-clear siren faded away with a heavy sigh. We were hungry and tired; it didn't occur to us we could have been killed.

We always had to walk and look, walk and look, even in bad times, even when there were only ugly things to look at. We roamed through the suburbs toward gray meadows strewn with fragments from anti-aircraft guns, meadows pockmarked with bomb craters. The roads were paths winding through the ruins, up and down the mountainside. On the slopes there were wood anemones, and at the foot of the hills there were entire houses with all their dead still inside. We walked along in poor shoes, our feet aching, but the sight of a pale morning glory raised our spirits, and we no longer saw the rubble they showed us but rather the first restored roofs, the first yellow window cushions, on which bloated women with ashen complexions rested their bosoms when they looked down in the street on holidays. We walked along the railroad tracks on which dark little clattering trains chugged away. Other trains passed through there as well, fast and brightly illuminated ones, which no one was allowed to board. Without stopping, they traversed the blighted countryside with the speed of the wind. We looked after them as we stood there huddled in our shabby coats and in shoes with torn soles, looking at each other's ghostly-green faces. We were okay; we talked about a future whose name was peace.

It is quite something that foreigners wish to walk to Marathon. The bus stops in the middle of nowhere—look at them, the poor souls, who don't know where to turn; there is no road. The sky was blue over Euboea, there was a thunder cloud over Hymettos, the storms of the equinox made their presence felt. In the struggling olive grove toward the bay, we found the tumulus, the mass grave; after thousands of years, this victory no longer glittered but manifested itself in autumn and melancholy. The old peasant from the farmstead nearby stood there relaxed, his mule with the bright almonds around its black eyes tearing off grass, his wife cooking porridge on the tripod next to the house wall. He gave us wine and olives and unsalted pretzels and showed us the way to the bay along a field of fluffy cotton. We left the olive trees by the ramshackle houses behind, the path petered out in thistles and thorns. Two purple thistle heads struggled for survival in a boggy ditch; a couple of stray dogs whimpered in the colorful little wooden stall, on whose door was written in an unsteady hand the words BAR OASIS. The magnificent bay shore was deserted, a primitive coast with dunes, full of washed up algae and plant material which had hardened and settled there to form mysteriously shaped gray ramparts. Surrounded by soft algae, we swam through these God-forsaken waters out toward the peninsula of Euboea; then we turned around, got dressed, and walked back to the road under patches of blue sky and black clouds rent by lightning. In the bleak wasteland of this isolated region we tried our best to grasp the wonder of the temple.

On the Ringstrasse we walked under the old trees: Schottentor, Bastei, University, Burgtheater, Rathaus, Bellaria, Hofburg, and Opera; the story of your youth and the stories about your youth, the kinds of pranks you used to play, one person taking the role of the inquisitive tourist, the other that of the helpful guide; only he would explain everything wrong: the Rathaus was the Residenz, the Opera was the University, until the persons going along got all mixed up and interrupted, feeling upset and sorry for themselves. Café Landtmann, where we sat in the evenings, having come from a distant part of the city that upset you. But here there was lots of space, lily-shaped lamps, gentle autumn air; and the path through the parks, all the roses in the Volksgarten still in bloom, and the massive public buildings, the domes and spires and the splendid iron knight, a rigid beauty in the moonlight. The road we took made all the difference to you. There were personal things connected with it and things that went far beyond the personal. You talked about the personal things, but these other things affected you, now that you had returned to your home town. In the palaces the candles flickered; they were staging concerts for the tourists, but you never wanted to attend; all you ever wanted to do was go for walks every night between the Opera and the Schottentor, back and forth like a sentry. For destiny ruled, a very personal and irreversible one, and if I had wished through some magic from the time I was young to become you for once and to see the world through your eyes, then I succeeded now that it was destroyed and the Rathaus spire with its iron knight shrouded in threatening black clouds vanished before your eyes. At this moment I was you, answering my own questions and seeing myself through your eyes, a helpless lover. Behind me the nightly torchlight procession leaving the Burg and mumbling death litanies moved toward us, prayers for the Habsburgers long since gone, prayers for the two of us. You didn't want to hear those. Unnerved and with long, unsteady steps you fled the scene and headed for the inner city with its narrow, comforting streets. After that everything changed. A road into darkness, and there was no longer a future.

And now we walk again in this unreal landscape on the narrow strips between water and water, sand beneath our feet, white dune sand that shifts and drifts. The fir trees bend with the sweeping winds, and across the inlet mythical beasts with heavy antlers move about with their springy gait. We sit in one of the skeleton houses left behind by the shifting dune, making patterns out of blue shells, cross and star. Sand is like time. It, too, drifts through us and finally leaves us behind like a pile of bare bones. But we don't give it a thought. We are dead, and above our heads the migratory birds screech.

Musical Chairs

In May of last year, a mysterious disease spread throughout the city, affecting the majority of the population during the following months. The doctors had no inkling as to what the nature and the cause of this disease might be. They treated the symptoms—the loss of strength and the extraordinary anxiety of the patients—with the usual restoratives and suppressants and waited, so it was said, for the first person to die so that based on the results they could perform an autopsy to further their research. Ill themselves, they tried in the meantime to comfort their patients, who, after all, were not bedridden; in fact, most of them appeared almost daily in their doctors' offices for fear they would miss out on a new remedy or some new information. The doctors assured their patients that although they might feel extremely weak and experience nervous ticking, they were in good shape and there was no reason for concern. As long as the doctors talked to them, all the patients were actually completely convinced of it. Their spirits rose, and they were even able to joke about the situation. But their high spirits did not last. As soon as they stepped out in the street and saw all the fearful faces there twitching with agitation, they slipped right back into their former state of depression and fear.

By early fall the mood in our city was ugly. Because of the possible danger of contagion, which continued to exist, nobody had been permitted to leave the city during the summer months, and this precaution had put us all in a state of deep depression. Many of us thought that all we would have needed to get well again was to get away—kind of like a seriously ill person stubbornly insisting on getting out of bed because he thinks he will be tormented there and there only. Death, in which most people saw their last salvation, still hadn't arrived, and we had started to watch each other and to scrutinize the faces of our closest friends for any shadow of the grim reaper.

The strange events that I want to recount occurred on three days during the month of October in my doctor's waiting room. Because of his infinite patience, he was sought out again and again by countless patients. On the first day, all the chairs were already taken by nine o'clock, and a lot of people were standing between the chairs. It was cold and damp outside. In the large front hall, which served as a waiting room, the light was on; on the coat hooks winter coats clung to winter coats while their owners huddled next to each other in grim silence. Suddenly a man who was not from the city, as I could tell from his accent, started to tell a story. Nobody wanted to listen to him; we weren't in the Orient after all, and what did people in our situation care about stories anyway? The man, who was standing all the way in the back of the room leaning against the wall, didn't let our angry whispering stop him. His voice, which at first had sounded just as weak and lifeless as ours, gradually became more forceful as he spoke, which caused both amazement and annoyance. I turned around and looked at him. He was pale like the rest of us, of medium height, middle-aged, and poorly dressed, and he had bright, inquisitive eyes like those of a child. What he related was repulsive, the story of a man in prison who is being devoured by rats and who ponders all kinds of other experiences, no less unpleasant. But the stubborn courage with which the narrator uttered these disgusting things finally made us all listen to him, attentively, even with a certain amount of excitement.

Because the office closed early that day, the same people more or less were in the waiting room the next day at the same time. The stranger, too, was there in the same spot as yesterday leaning against the paneled wall. When he started to look as if he were about to come up with some more stories, he immediately had an attentive audience that received every newcomer with angry hissing as in a theater or at a concert. But it soon turned out that this time the stranger, whether out of weakness or a lack of desire, wasn't even thinking of telling a story. He uttered a word, made a long pause, uttered another word, made another pause, and so on. It was not particularly entertaining, since these words were not related to each other at all and were not special in any way—a mishmash so to speak—and it is hard to understand why we listened so attentively to him and why everyone who was called into the doctor's office got up reluctantly, almost unwillingly. Apparently it stemmed from the fact that each separately pronounced word evoked certain memories in us, perhaps even raised hopes. The word was somehow left hanging there all by itself, thereby becoming enlarged and very weighty.

The next day the mood in the waiting room was cheerful, indeed almost joyous. The stranger had thought of a game he wanted to play with us and had already begun to give directions. This game required the use of quite a few chairs, some of which had to be dragged in from the doctor's dining room. I suddenly remembered a game in which someone was supposed to start playing a song on the piano and then suddenly stop. Then everybody had to find a seat, only there wouldn't be room for everyone, a chair would be missing. Crazy, I thought. Something like that in a waiting room? Are we children or something? But I didn't say anything. I got in line and started to walk around the row of chairs with the others; there was no piano there. The stranger drummed his fingers on a gong, which apparently was also a part of the doctor's dining room furnishings, a fascinating and terrifying rhythm. We moved forward, giggling, whispering, and then silently, faster, faster yet, tripping, scraping, constantly hoping that the drumming would stop. When that happened, we all rushed for the chairs, no longer happy but fearful and angry as if getting a seat were a matter of life and death. Then suddenly everyone was sitting down, nobody stood, there wasn't any chair missing at all. How could that be? Because the stranger had collapsed, because he was lying stretched out on the floor near the door, dead.

It has been almost a year since the day we played that childish game in the doctor's waiting room. The disease is practically conquered, even the most stubborn cases are improving. It is possible but not quite certain that our city may owe its salvation to this first death, to the storyteller and wordsayer no less. It may also be that at precisely that moment somewhere in an entirely different part of the world, in America or Australia, a cure for the mysterious disease was discovered. After all, they have been working on it for quite some time. But even if that is the case, I'll think of the mysterious stranger often. I'll try to recollect his unpleasant story and catch myself rapping my fingers on the table, recapturing the fascinating rhythm of his drum. I'll try hard to write down the words that he uttered between long pauses: blackberry brambles—rain—ice flower—midnight ... Is it really possible that there wasn't something else involved?

Christine

I can't begin to describe the way my husband has been acting lately, the way he just sits there all quiet in the middle of the room staring into space and looking right through you as if there were nothing there, not even a body with arms and legs and a dress and an apron, let alone his own wife. "For God's sake, George," I say, trying to sound cheerful, "snap out of it. Why don't you go out in the garden; the roses need to be covered, they say it's going to freeze tonight." Of course, I could do that myself or have one of the children do it; I'm not one of these wives who make their husbands do chores, and he has never done the dishes. But I don't like the fact that he calls in sick when he isn't sick at all and that he sits around the house and gets weird ideas, for I know what kind of ideas those are, not what you might think, although maybe what you think after all. But it isn't that simple, it isn't that ordinary ...

That simple, that ordinary! A man of about fifty, the father of four with a wife who is a little broad around the hips. He simply can't imagine he could ever have been madly in love, and if he does think about it, he's embarrassed. But to be madly in love again, that's what he would like to be, to be in his prime once more, even if just in his imagination, indeed better if just in his imagination, because everything is too much trouble anyway; the wife is watching, and the children are watching; the children are grown. Thoughts like that go through your head when you sit on the beach with the whole family, the picnic basket in front of you, and watch the girls on the diving board. Or by the window in the evening, when the stores are closing and the girls walk down the street arm in arm. That's the way it is with men when they reach fifty. It passes, no need to get all upset about it; it's better to pretend you don't notice a thing. But I do get upset when my husband stands by the window and even more so when he sits in the middle of the room, without a newspaper, without anything. I get upset because I know what's behind it, know it's not fear of getting old but the memory of a particular event.

"Do what you can to make your husband forget about this whole thing as soon as possible, Frau Bornemann," said the doctor, our family physician whom we really had only for the children, because the two of us were never sick. After all, we were still young, thirty-eight and thirty-two years old, and the children were still small. My husband was already working for Gütermann at that point, and he still is. But we didn't live here then. We lived in a housing development in the suburbs, a lower middle-class neighborhood, little row houses that start to deteriorate before they are even completed. Soon after what happened happened—and I'll get to that in a moment—we moved away. I insisted on it; after all, there was nothing there, just the same old postage-stamp lot with its bed of asters in the front yard and the wrought-iron fence, which the girl clutched with her little hands, blue from the cold. A strand of her white-blond hair clung to that fence for the longest time, and nobody could bring himself to remove it and get rid of it.

Of course, you'll think it was one of our children whose hair caught on the iron fence out there and that that's what my husband couldn't forget. But it wasn't one of ours. Our children are all grown; they have always been in good physical shape and done well in school and been a pleasure to be around. Why, even my husband enjoyed them, and he never looked at them the way he looks at them now, with such indifference and reluctance, even with an expression of disgust sometimes, the way you look at an animal, a pesky, repulsive animal ...

That was about ten days ago; in fact, it is exactly ten days ago. It was a Sunday, and because we have a car now, we frequently go away for the whole day although we would sometimes prefer to stay home, and the children would rather sleep late and hang out with their friends in the afternoon. At breakfast we discuss where we would like to go, and as soon as the subject comes up, we always get into an argument. The boys are grouchy because they haven't had enough sleep, and the girls' faces are covered with cold cream because they claim their skin needs a rest on Sundays. They all stretch and yawn, and my husband sits there with the map in front of him making one suggestion after another, and somebody always has an objection: there's no water, there are no woods, this place is boring, and that one doesn't have enough going on. I try to be the mediator, and I'm also the one who reminds the children not to talk with food in their mouths and not to wad up their napkins and toss them on the table. But I don't take it all too seriously, and my husband never took it too seriously either, only on this particular day everything made him angry and upset. He said something about dirty fingernails and commented that Judith was too heavy to wear slacks. Needless to say, the children were up in arms. Beppo asked how he could be expected to keep his nails clean if he had to haul up coals from the basement, and Judith wanted to know just who she got those extra pounds around the hips from, adding that Mom was pretty well padded herself. That's true enough, and it's also true that the children are a bit overweight and don't have the best shapes in the world, and they do have thick fingers and broad faces. But that's really not their fault. It's not their fault, and it's no reason for my husband to do

105

what he did that day—I mean, get up and throw the map down and scream "for this, for this"—and storm out of the room.

Of course, by now I know very well what these words "for this, for this" actually meant. But at that time I didn't know. I stayed at the table and consoled the children, although they were not that affected by the incident. In fact, Uwe, the youngest, even mumbled something like "not quite all there." That was a smart-alecky remark all right, and it hurt because I felt something really wasn't quite right. We finally drove off by ourselves that Sunday, without the children. We took a walk in the woods and stopped for coffee somewhere. My husband was quiet and depressed the whole time. When we sat at the outdoor café, where a group of happy young people had gathered for an afternoon of boating and dancing, he began to observe the girls again, not like someone who is looking for a fling but seriously and attentively, as if he were looking for someone, some particular person. Then a young girl with loose white-blond hair and a delicate, almost translucent face suddenly walked past our table, holding hands with a young man the way people do these days. My husband sat up straight and looked closely at the girl; then he dropped his face in his hands and said in a voice that sounded broken and harsh and desperate: "That could be she." And now I suddenly knew what he meant and why he had said "for this, for this" that morning, and I realized all my efforts over the years had been in vain.

All my efforts, that sounds so solemn and smacks of plans and intentions. But I never had any plans or intentions. Away, I thought then, out of this apartment, away from this neighborhood, from our friends, to the other side of town. That was something to strive for and something to do, and soon I started to look for other goals and pastimes. I was not after money; I had been quite happy in the cheap apartment, and I wasn't ambitious for my husband either; just so he earned enough money to see the children through school. But now I started to encourage him to move up, to try for a management position, and so he would pour over his books in the evenings, and he really liked that a lot. When he actually did become a manager a few years later, we celebrated his promotion with a glass of wine that evening and even woke up the children and let them drink to his success. I thought about our family doctor from the old neighborhood again, and I looked at my husband and thought he had forgotten that old business. We were over the hump. But now I knew we had never gotten over the hump, because the words "for this, for this" meant "for these children, for this wife, for this family life I have shouldered a guilt which no human being can ever absolve me of." When my husband said "that could be she" when he saw this beautiful, frail girl in the outdoor café, he was thinking of the child that was strangled that time in front of our garden gate and that had cried out for help so pitifully just moments before.

Of course, there can't be any question of guilt on my husband's part. If anyone is guilty at all, it's me. I told my husband this a hundred times over when the police came and he had what amounted to a nervous breakdown: stiff eyes, trembling hands, and bubbles of saliva around his mouth. I told the police the same thing, and they tried to calm my husband down. They said they thought we would just have to appear as witnesses, and indeed we did appear as witnesses at the trial, and nobody ever blamed my husband. We simply had to tell what happened, this, that, and the other. My husband was home that day because he had been sick, not the way he is now but physically ill. This was his first day out of bed, and he stands there by the window, and I'm clearing the table and happen to look out the window. The girl comes running down the sidewalk, a thin girl with white-blond hair, someone we don't know, and a tall heavy-set man whom we don't know either is right behind her. The girl sees us, or at least my husband, and begins to scream and rattle our garden gate, but it's closed; and the tall, heavy-set man throws himself on the girl, reaches under her white hair from behind, and puts his hands around her throat. Between the girl's first cry for help and her eventual silence, several minutes elapse during which my husband turns around and starts to run out the door. He can't because I'm clinging to him and holding on to his sleeve with a claw-like grip so he can't shake me off. "Don't go," I beg, hoarse with fear and worry. "Think of the children, don't go." Because I say that, my husband, who might have been able to tear himself away, stops for a moment, just long enough for the stranger out there to wring the screaming little bird's neck. We recounted all this at the trial, and we also learned a number of things: that the child's name was Christine, that she was seven years old, and that she had been living on our street for only a few days. We also learned that the man, the murderer, was crazy and thought the whole world was out to get him. A few minutes before, he had been hounded by some different children and thought he wanted to take revenge or had to protect himself from something or other. But now I ask you—what business was that actually of *ours*?

"What is it to you?" I said to my husband then, and I also said that lots of children die, even while they're still young: they are run over by a car, or they get polio or tuberculosis; children die and grownups die, there's no end to it. Every second of the day somebody dies somewhere. Every second someone breathes his last breath, and if he isn't clutching the rails of a garden fence, then he's clutching a sheet or the earth or the hand that's trying to wipe the perspiration from his forehead. It is some people's fate to die young, I say, and who knows what would have happened to the girl, maybe something much worse. Even though I carried her into the house myself that time and held her little panic-stricken face to my breast, I still believe that. Some people will undoubtedly think ill of me for that, but I can't help the fact that my husband means more to me than a strange little girl whose name is Christine. I can't help the fact that during the whole trial I saw only his pale, helpless face and that because I was so angry, I couldn't think of anything other than why did this have to happen to us? Why did the girl have to be walking on our side of the street when she lived on the other side, the side with the uneven numbers? Why did the madman have to catch up with her right in front of our garden gate? Why did it happen to be a day when my husband was home, and why did we have to be in the living room when we are usually out in the kitchen at that hour? Why did things have to happen in such a way that my husband is haunted by the thought that he could have saved the girl ... ?

I guess I know now that nothing—his promotion in the company, getting a house of our own, and living the good life—can dispel this notion of his. I know he hates me for holding on to him that day, and he hates the children for being alive and healthy and strong. Since that Sunday when we drove out in the woods, I've been watching him constantly, and sometimes I get so angry I could shake him. "Wake up, for God's sake," I want to scream. "Those are morbid dreams. What will it lead to if we let things get to us? I can tell by looking at you what it will lead to: loneliness, melancholy, being 'not quite all there.' 'All there,' after all, means taking things the way they come and making the best of them and not chasing a phantom, someone you didn't even know, someone who has been gone for ten years."

But there are times when I think it isn't really guilt that haunts and torments my husband. I think the dead girl represents something like grace and beauty for its own sake. Because she died so young and wasn't really touched by the world, she stayed that way, so graceful and so innocent. And then I secretly admit that for women everything must make sense and have meaning, but men are allowed to follow their dreams and be saddened by the madness and the imperfection of this world. I admit this, in private, as I just did again when I stepped out in the garden and saw my husband standing there. He had actually covered the roses with pine boughs and old burlap bags. Right now he is examining the birch tree, which has been attacked by something or other that makes the leaves curl up, and he looks unhappy. I look at him and love him as never before in my entire life, not even in the first years of our marriage. But I wouldn't dare tell him that. So I simply touch his arm, very lightly, and say thanks, and he turns around, surprised, but not unfriendly.

Foreign Territory

You hear so much about anxiety these days, about this strange malaise that doesn't just come on suddenly but seems to be a condition. Somehow it's like sitting there in the dark with your hair standing on end, and yet there is nothing really wrong, except maybe there's nothing there at all anymore, no floor, no wall, only you, sitting in your chair, with clenched fingers and your hair standing on end ...

Not that these objects actually disappear; they just become unreal. Somehow they lose their meaning, and their shape is distorted. Right within our own four walls we are surrounded by ghosts, by fog, by nothingness. Before we know it, we resemble someone visiting a country whose language he doesn't understand, some eerie, totally foreign country.

I might never have found out what that means if I hadn't met the two pilots. I guess we're all pretty conditioned these days. We have looked death in the eye, as it were, whenever we chose not to duck or throw ourselves in a ditch. Or at least, if we did, we got right up again and went on our merry way.

I am sure the two men that I want to tell about have surmounted much greater dangers than any of us. They had undoubtedly flown off course many times, getting into storms or ice clouds or flak that tore the wings of their planes to shreds. Yet these two brave men sat next to me one fall evening after the war was over beside themselves with fear. I kept looking at them, and I finally understood what it meant, this foreign territory, this foreign land.

You've got to know them, these late fall evenings where I live. You must have come to know how the forests, which are so beautiful and colorful during the daytime, red and gold, can suddenly become black and alien. Just a few minutes ago they were part of the meadows, these golden fjords that stretch up into the mountains and to the vineyards, now heavy with grapes, along the glacial stream. But the moment night falls, they are just a part of the vast forests that cover the mountains. The winds that pass through them come from deep valleys far away, and the sounds that stir in the thicket have nothing whatsoever to do with the peaceful sounds in the dusky villages.

Needless to say, those of us who have walked the twisting paths a hundred times over in the daytime also manage to find our way around at night. But how would that be possible for two men who arrive in the area for the first time? Two men who out of sheer boredom drove off in their car, away from the city where they sat around in an office issuing certificates when they were dying to be up in their planes, to be a part of this strangely intense military life.

At first everything went fairly well. It was still light; even in the middle of the forest every little leaf was clearly recognizable. Up there by the little spring house, where you can look out over the whole river valley across to the sister peaks, they turned off the highway and drove up the timber trail, one turn and then another, not very far at all. They had taken a rifle with them, and now they got out. The lieutenant put his key in his pocket and slammed the doors shut; the sergeant carried his rifle. They went up a little ravine and sat down somewhere on a raised hide, in any case not in a clearing, because there are no clearings in this forest. Incidentally, there hasn't been any game there for quite a while. But the foreigners had no way of knowing that. So they sat there listening and waiting, and very soon it got dark, much sooner than they had expected. The lieutenant lit a cigarette, and the sergeant did, too. They were old air force buddies, and for a while they sat like that next to each other on the tree trunk feeling really good because it wasn't anything like the city but much more like the airfield when they would sit there waiting for take-off. Of course, there you could always hear voices and the sound of engines and see green and red lights, but here it was terribly dark and still. For that reason the lieutenant suddenly got up and threw his cigarette away, and then they started walking, but not quite in the right direction. There was a stretch of new forest ahead of them now, a plantation of fir trees, which they had trouble getting through, and a slope with blackberries whose thorns scratched their hands. It took them a quarter of an hour, no doubt, until they reached the highway again, and in the meantime they got pretty angry: this damned forest, this damned country. Then they suddenly stopped because not only did they feel the highway underneath their feet, they also recognized it now, the hairpin curve and the car that was parked there, an unshapely black mass on a gray winding ribbon. It was probably at that moment they were overcome with fear.

Of course, I can't say exactly what happened up there. I only know how it is in the forest at night sometimes, how a wind can suddenly spring up, God only knows from where, and how something will be rustling as if whole packs of spooky creatures were streaming through the underbrush; how everything becomes shadows and blackness, only the shadows are not calm but fidget and dart about like someone who's up to no good and who therefore is trying to hide. But I am quite certain the two men, who knew only the expanse of the firmament, suddenly started to see ghosts as they stood there in the dark forest. A gust of wind sprang up, the leaves rustled, shadows moved around the car. One can imagine all sorts of things, and that's apparently exactly what the two men did. Otherwise they surely wouldn't have left their car in the forest and raced down the mountain, down the timber trail at break-neck speed to the spring house, and finally down the highway until they reached our village. They wouldn't have gone to the mayor and asked him to go up in the mountains and get their car. The mayor wouldn't have sent for us to smooth relations, as he put it, although the truth was that he was afraid to leave his wife alone. And we wouldn't have sat in his kitchen with the strangers for over an hour, most of this time in total silence.

In the beginning, of course, we exchanged a few words. The foreigners stood in the middle of the room, short fellows in shabby uniforms, ominous looking, not at all kindly disposed. We explained why we were there, and the lieutenant told his story. "There was someone there in the forest," he said. "There was someone by my car, I saw it clearly."

"And who might that have been?" I asked surprised.

"I guess you would know that better than I," the lieutenant said, looking at me angrily. Then we translated what he had said, he handed the mayor his keys, and the mayor got out of there in a hurry. Actually he was a brave man, he was just concerned for his wife, who was sitting in the bedroom quiet as a mouse. After all, he had no way of knowing that the foreigners never gave her any thought at all, nor did they think of any other woman in the whole world.

"Won't you sit down?" I asked after a while.

The two men exchanged a quick glance. Then they sat down next to each other on the one side of the bench, which stood diagonally across from us, and Carl and I sat down on the other side and put our hands on the bare table. I noticed that the lieutenant already had a few gray hairs and that the sergeant had a finger missing on his right hand. I also noticed that Carl was making a polite face but that he was uncomfortable sitting there like a defendant or a hostage. We were visiting someone in the village. When all was said and done, what did this whole story have to do with us? At my wits' end, I started to rack my brain over how I could get the three men to talk to one another.

It's not too much fun just to sit there and stare at each other for any length of time and never move a muscle. After all, we are all human beings. We could talk about food or about the weather, and we would soon find out that we have an immortal soul. But if we just keep quiet, I thought, fear has free range. It spreads from one person or from two. It seems to have very definite characteristics, but actually it is just unfamiliarity gaining ground and distorting everything. You take a close look at something, a human face, for example, and suddenly it comes apart: one eye hovers in the ceiling, the other is completely lifeless, you have two or three noses, your chin is down in your chest like a pointed rock. When you look out the window, the houses are caving in and spreading out like black cowpies with vermin crawling underneath. You listen to the ticking of the kitchen clock; every sweet tone of the pendulum becomes a terrifying stroke like that of a world clock that is never silenced.

I was already getting close to giving myself over to the strange atmosphere that was starting to spread between us. But then I noticed something on the lieutenant's uniform that looked like an airman's insignia. This discovery didn't make the man any more likable in my eyes, but it did bring me back to the world of reality. Well, well, now, a pilot, I thought. A guy who goes up in a plane and drops bombs, then turns around and lands and drinks and shoots at his own reflection in the mirror. Good night! Then my thoughts went in a different direction, and without wanting to, I spoke the name that was on the tip of my tongue.

Not everyone may be familiar with this name. It was the name of a man who flew when planes were still wobbly little boxes and when radio communications were inadequate, to say the least, and who has recounted his experiences in a wonderfully simple and human way. Thus he has become the voice of all those who have seen the sun rise out of the middle of the ocean and the rainbow sweep across the steppes, of those who have thought that sights like that would make man better—freer and kinder at the same time. And also the voice of all those whose throats have gotten hoarse from drinking because they couldn't find any other way of bridging the terrible abyss between heaven and earth.

"St. Exupéry," I said in the quiet room.

When the foreigners heard this name, life returned to their stony faces.

"Did you know him?" the lieutenant asked distrustfully.

"I've read his books," I said.

"I haven't read his books," said the lieutenant. "But I was on his staff."

"Really?" I asked surprised.

"Yes," the lieutenant said sternly.

"Is it true he's dead?" I asked.

"He was also on his staff," the lieutenant said, looking at the sergeant.

"He didn't return," the sergeant said. "He went up one day and didn't ever return."

"They never found him?" Carl asked.

"No," said the lieutenant.

"At least not yet," the sergeant said.

Then there was silence again for a while, but it was a different kind of silence from before. I thought about the books I had read, trying to remember different details: the dance around the Horn of Salamanca, the black tiara of flak above the flames of Arras. But all this was not as indelibly imprinted on my mind as the character of the sensitive little boy in his last enchanting book, this child who learns the agony of love and who seeks consolation in friendship.

"It was at the very end," said the lieutenant, starting to tell about the last days of the war, and whenever he paused, I heard the voice of the little planetary wanderer who gains a fox for a friend here on earth. J'en ai fait mon ami et il est maintenant unique au monde, said the little prince.

"Maybe he suffered material damage," Carl said.

On ne voit bien qu'avec le coeur, the little prince said.

"But surely they would have found him," said the lieutenant, resting his head in his hand.

I no longer joined in the conversation, but it didn't matter anymore. The men had started talking to each other, they no longer looked down at their chests or at their hands but into each other's eyes, and in the middle of the room stood the late pilot like a flame casting its beautiful glow over our faces. But then something happened that extinguished and drove away this delicate glow of humanity in the most disgraceful way.

For I suddenly remembered I still had things to do. After all, we had become human beings once again, human beings who had plans and something to do. I had a small debt to settle at the house next door; I could take care of that pretty fast, and now that we were such good friends, I guess I could come and go as I pleased.

I whispered to Carl what I had in mind and reached across the table for him to give me some money. Carl reached in his coat pocket, since he carried his bills and coins around in it loose, but to be able to get the money out of his pocket, he first had to take out an object and put it down in front of him. This object was a flashlight, an unwieldy field-gray thing that dropped rather heavily on the table with a rattling sound.

At this sound there was a short violent movement. The two men suddenly jumped up; it sounded as if they were completely armored, but they suddenly just stood there with revolvers in their hands. Needless to say, we, too, jumped up, and the four of us stood very close across from each other, silent and breathing rapidly. Then the lieutenant caught sight of the flashlight on the table, and he dropped his hand and said: "Sit down." But even so we all just stood there immobile, staring at each other.

At that moment we heard the hum of the car outside, which the mayor had picked up and driven down the mountain. His house was located on a hill, and we could clearly hear him shifting into low gear to get into the courtyard. When he stepped into the room, we had all long since returned from those regions where everything comes apart, where the world clock continues its horrible course and where one person kills the other without knowing why. We could probably have shaken hands and wished each other good night. But we left very quickly, without looking at each other or saying another word.

The Deserter

About six o'clock in the evening the day before Easter—the bells which are said to spend Good Friday in Rome could return any moment now—about six o'clock, as I said, Marian heard the deserter, her husband and lover, come up the cellar steps. She got the key out of her apron pocket and unlocked the cellar door, but when her husband tried to step into the room, she put both hands on his chest and pushed him away.

"You can't come in just now," she said, "not today, not right now."

Her husband stood in the dark, his blue eyes flashing angrily, his hands covered with blood.

"What's wrong?" he asked.

"There are people in the woods," Marian said. "They are standing over there by the slope looking in this direction. The children played their pipes. Didn't your hear them?"

"I heard them," her husband said. "But I can't stand it down there. I've got to wash my hands. They are covered with blood."

"Did you butcher the lamb?" Marian asked.

"Yes," her husband said, and pushing her aside, he went over to the sink and ran the water.

"Did the lamb squeal?" Marian asked.

"No," said her husband. "It didn't feel a thing."

"And the children?" asked Marian. "Did they notice anything?"

"No," said the husband. He had sent the children to the village, and before that he had colored Easter eggs for them, beautiful eggs with yellow mountains on them and big, blue rivers, scenery just as it was where he came from, which is to say America. There was a lot of water between here and there, and Marian had never seen that country. She ought to have a look at the eggs now to see how pretty they were, he said. They were sitting in a dish covered with a plate, and her husband removed the plate. But Marian didn't even glance in that direction; instead she looked out the window.

"Quick, Jim, quick," she said listening to the wind that blew there all the time and sometimes turned into a storm that sounded as if all hell had broken loose. But this time it blew very gently, its sack full of bells still silent.

"What's with you, Marian?" the husband asked.

115

"It's Franz," Marian said. "He came all the way up to the woods with them. He tried to talk me into marrying him. If I don't, he wants an explanation."

Irritated, her husband pushed back the dish with the eggs.

"Why don't you?" he said. "You would have a good life. A husband who can be seen. Not a vagabond, not a cross-country runner who comes and goes in the night."

"Don't talk like that," Marian said. "Help me stretch the wool. No one has as good a life as I do. A husband all to myself."

She set up the knitting frame and got the wool and the pattern out of her bag, the work she brought home from the knitting factory every week.

"But how about you?" she said.

"What about me?" her husband wanted to know.

For him, Marian said, starting to stretch the red and blue strands, it was always the same. The same bit of sky, the same forest edge, and the high meadows for catching a breath of fresh air at night.

"Is everything that different every day?" the husband said in a grumpy tone of voice. "Every day we move a little bit closer to summer or to winter. The beech tree behind the house is already budding."

But it really was a lot like being in prison, his wife answered. There was no other man for him to talk to. He had no voice in the community, and he never learned anything new.

"I read the paper," the husband said. "I listen to the radio. I know where we're headed. When there's a change, the foxes leave their holes."

"I don't understand you," Marian said looking at him anxiously. It was getting dark now, and in front of the window you could hear the voices of the children, whom Marian had taught to say that there was nobody living in the house other than they and their mother. She had also taught them to play their little pipes as soon as anyone got close to the isolated house in the woods.

"Someone has made the people down in the village suspicious," Marian said. "They say a man is hiding out in the woods, and he is supposed to have stolen the town clerk's chickens and the washing off the line from the school master's wife. They also say somebody has been poaching, and they found a man beaten to death behind the saw mill."

"I didn't do it," the husband said angrily.

"Of course you didn't," Marian said. "But someone must have seen you in the woods at night. Now they want to get the authorities up here, and they will be bringing their dogs with them. Won't you please go down in the cellar and hide in the tunnel. I'll lock the door."

"If that's the way things are," the man said, looking straight at her, "then I'm definitely not going down there. I'll sit down by you and wait for Easter. You know why."

"Why?" Marian asked putting the knitting frame away, since all she could see now was the golden streak of evening sky that filled the window.

"You aren't thinking, Marian," said her husband. "Go get the candlestick and put candles in it. I'm sure you remember."

"I do," Marian said distressed. "It was Easter. But Easter fell late that year."

"Yes," her husband said. "It was a late Easter and an early spring. The lilacs were full of delicate little leaves, the chestnuts full of pale little hands reaching for the moist blue sky."

Marian had placed the candlestick on the table and sat down now with her hands in her lap. She thought of that spring and saw the village children playing with their tops and whips on the street in front of the city hall. She also saw the flock of sheep and all the newborn lambs, spots of white in the undulating gray wool, coming down the valley. She saw the buttercups and spearwort and the meadow paths with their blue puddles, which a dazzling hot sun dried up almost instantly.

"There was all kinds of commotion in the streets," the husband said. "We had just moved into new quarters a short time ago and were supposed to leave again. The sirens howled. Commands were shouted. People scrambled from house to house."

"Yes," Marian thought and looked at her husband who had been quartered at her house then, this young, foreign soldier, whose socks she had washed and whose knapsack she had packed. Before he left, she had poured him a glass of wine, and he had offered her bread, and they had eaten and drunk together, their lips trembling with grief and disbelief.

"The bells started to toll," she said. "You waved as you walked away."

"'Come back soon' you shouted," said the husband, "laughing through your tears. And I really did come back—that same night."

"We stood here by the window as they were leaving down there," Marian said. "We heard the heavy engines of the trucks and the wheels of the tanks."

"I tried to make out the dimmed lights," the husband said. "I listened for the voices of my friends. But you hid my head on your shoulder."

Marian sat up straight because just then she heard the sound of a little reed. She also thought she heard strange dogs barking farther down in the valley. She got up quickly, positioned herself behind her husband, and pressed his head to her bosom.

"Do it again," she said desperately. "Hide your head. Close your eyes." With these words she tried to put her hands over her husband's eyes like a bandage, but her husband reached for her hands, pulled them down, and refused to let go.

"We can't go on like this, Marian," he said. "There's a time to hide and a time to come out of hiding; there's a time to be silent and a time to speak up."

"What are you trying to tell me, Jim?" Marian asked frightened.

"I want to have my say in a court of law," her husband said. "I want to let them know why I've been living here underground and what I've been doing all these years."

"They'll never believe you," Marian said. "They'll say you've become an oddball. They'll say that someone who spent seven years inside a mountain is bound to have lost his mind."

She went and got the matches from the stove and lighted the candles in the Easter candlestick. In the candlelight her husband's face seemed so strange to her that she wondered if he really had lost his mind. But just then her husband started laughing happily. He got up and moved the table and asked her to sit down behind it.

"I'll answer with logic, tell my story with reason, and defend myself with cunning. Watch me, I'll show you how. You be the judge."

"I can't," Marian said nervously and drew the curtains. She heard quite clearly now people with dogs coming up the narrow valley, and she thought of her children who didn't dare leave their posts and undoubtedly couldn't figure out why their father didn't hurry down in the cellar and from there into the old silver mine, where it was safe.

"Then I'll be the judge myself," the husband said. "I'll be the judge and the defendant and the bailiff. 'Enter,' I call. 'Bring in the defendant, Jim Croyden.' And now I enter and sit down in the dock."

"Stop it, Jim," his wife pleaded. "You have no time to lose."

"Now I'll be the judge," said Jim. "See my robe and my mortarboard? I'm sitting up here with a bell in front of me. Ding-a-ling, goes the bell. 'Name?' I ask, and the defendant states his name. 'Occupation?' I ask, and the defendant says 'Writer,' and I say 'Is that a fact!' Then I ring the bell again: Ding-a-ling. 'Why,' I ask, 'why did the defendant desert his troop during the last spring of our glorious war?'"

The husband sat on the table. There was something fanatic about his eyes, and his voice sounded foreign and unnatural.

"Now you be the audience," he whispered hitting Marian hard on the shoulder. "Be the audience and boo!"

But Marian wrested herself from his grip. "I don't want to, Jim," she sobbed. "I don't want to be anybody else. I'm your wife."

"Then at least listen," her husband said angrily. "Look, maybe they'll even let you peek in when they put me in the electric chair. There's a little window in the door."

"Jim!" Marian said outraged.

"Let's continue," Jim said, sitting down on the table again. "'Please answer the question,' the judge says. 'Why did you desert your troop and hide out at the house of a girl by the name of Marian?'

"'For love,'" I'll say.

"'Come on,' the judge says. 'You did it because you were a coward.'

"'That's true, too,' I'll say. 'Cowardess was part of it.'

"'So I was right,' the judge says. 'You didn't want to die.'"

The husband sat on top of the table and moved his arms, and Marian thought the children would burst into the room any moment now, the authorities on their heels, the police in their uniforms. She also thought that at least the candles ought to be extinguished, because she could already imagine her husband's shadow dancing on the curtain so that everybody could see it from afar. But she didn't blow out the candles; she didn't do anything. She just sat there on the kitchen bench looking straight at her husband.

"'You didn't want to die,' the judge says," continued her husband. "And I'll say 'I didn't want to kill,' and then I'll say 'I had a dream then, judge.'

"'What kind of dream?' the judge asks reluctantly.

"'In my dream I stood by my machine gun,' I say, 'and across from me was the whole enemy army. All the soldiers were lined up next to one another on the ridge. There was no cover at all, nothing but dark little men against the red sun, and nobody moved.'

"'Hahaha,' says the judge. 'I bet that was fine with you.'

"'No, Your Honor,' I answer, 'that wasn't fine with me at all. For at that point I fired, and all the soldiers were killed. But everyone who fell got up again and walked right through me, and each one of them left something behind inside me, a bit of life and a bit of death.'

"'Don't give me any of that,' says the judge. 'You were afraid, that's all there's to it.'

"'Sure,' I say. 'I was scared just as they'll be scared in any new war. They'll get over their fear and gain nothing. Or they'll run away and gain nothing.'

"'I see,' says the judge. 'So you admit you gained nothing by your desertion?' And I'll say 'Yes, I admit that, for I've raised children who will have to kill, too.'

"'So you regret what you've done?' says the judge, and I'll say 'No, I have no regrets. For I've shown my children how the starlings muster up courage to take their first flight and how the snowdrops with their delicate flowers push through the hard soil to reach the light. I've told them how many scientists have risked their lives to make the human race healthier and happier, and how a man by the name of Odysseus endured countless adventures on the seas to make it home again. I've lived seven years giving love and receiving love. The love one has given or received is never lost in the world.'"

With these words, which the husband had uttered loudly, indeed fervently, he collapsed and dropped his face in his hands.

"Don't say any more," Marian said, throwing her arms around his neck. The husband cleared his throat and reached for a cigarette, which he lighted with the Easter candle, and when he started to speak, his old matter-of-fact voice and his old boyish face were back again.

"Ours has been a strange marriage," he said. "But maybe it wasn't any stranger than other marriages. In every marriage you try to be alone with the other person and to hide from the world. You try to give your children something to take with them, the best thing you've got. Then one day the world is at your doorstep shouting 'Hands up' and 'Come on out with your hands above your head,' and you walk out with your hands above your head."

"But everything is really just a terrible misunderstanding," Marian said. "You didn't steal the wash, and you didn't kill anyone. What you did would soon have been water over the dam, and then we could have left for your country, happy and free." She began to cry, and her husband turned around and wiped the tears from her face with his fingers.

"We're constantly underway," he said conciliatorily. "Every bud is a station, and every brown autumn leaf is a station. But as far as that other business is concerned, everything is just a misunderstanding, all the hatred and all the misery in the world."

"We always did understand each other," Marian said sobbing.

"Yes," her husband said, "at least, that's something. That will remain even when those who love each other are separated and thrust out into what to them must seem like eternal night. It will remain behind and drift through the air like the fine seeds which, illuminated by the sun, drop by their parachutes through the shadows of the forest."

Just then the children started to play their pipes shrilly out there, and now you could hear steps on the stone path along with voices and the panting of big dogs being led on a leash and straining at their leashes.

"Hurry up and hide," Marian whispered frightened. But her husband jumped up from the table, and without kissing her or looking at her one last time, he rushed toward the door. He tore it open, and just then the curtains started to billow and the candles to flicker, and lights and shadows danced through the kitchen. Marian jumped up and tried to run after her husband. But at this point Jim, who was standing in the doorway, was already raising his hands above his head. The dogs barked, and down there in the village the bells, which had just returned from Rome, announced it was Easter.

Thaw

The apartment was on the third floor of a large bright apartment building. The rooms were bright and friendly as well, blue linoleum with white speckles, a walnut cabinet with glass doors, and armchairs with foam rubber cushions in bright-red covers. Although the kitchen was old-fashioned, it was freshly painted, snow-white and cozy, with a built-in bench and a large table. Outside it was thawing. The snow was melting and dripping from the gutter; big clumps of it slid off the sloping roof, sending its powder past the window. The wife was in the kitchen, and her husband was just coming home from work. It was almost six o'clock and starting to get dark. She heard him unlock the front door from the outside and then lock it again from the inside; she heard him use the bathroom, come back, open the door behind her, and say hi. Only then did she remove her hands from the soapy water, in which her hose lay like twisting eels. She rinsed her fingers, turned around, and nodded at him.

"Did you lock the door?" she asked.

"Yes," said her husband.

"Twice?" asked the wife.

"Yes," said her husband.

The wife went to the window and lowered the shutter.

"Don't turn the light on yet," she said. "There's a crack in the shutter. You had better nail a piece of cardboard over it."

"You're too jittery," said the husband.

He went out and came back with some tools and a piece of heavy cardboard. A picture had been glued to one side of the cardboard, a black man with a red scarf and gleaming teeth, and her husband nailed the cardboard on so that you could see the black man from the inside. He worked by the scanty light that shone into the kitchen from the hall, and he was barely done before his wife came and turned out the hall light and closed the door. The fluorescent light above the stove jerked and flickered; suddenly the room was brightly lit, and the husband went over to the sink, washed his hands under the faucet, and sat down at the table.

"Now let's have something to eat," he said.

"Fine," said his wife.

She got a platter with sausage, ham, and dill pickles out of the refrigerator and put a dish of potato salad next to it. The bread, in a pretty basket, was already on the table, which was covered with a linen-look oilcloth with cheerful little boats on it.

"Did you get a paper?" the wife asked.

"Yes," the husband said. He went out in the hall again, came back, and put the newspaper on the table.

"You've got to close the door," the wife said. "The light shines right through the glass door onto the stairs; it's obvious we're home. Anything in the paper?" she asked.

"There's something about the back side of the moon," the husband said. He had closed the door and sat down again and was now starting in on his potato salad and sausage. "There was also something about China and Algiers."

"I don't care about that," the wife said. "What I want to know is whether or not the police are going to do anything."

"Yes," said her husband. "They've drawn up a list."

"A list," said the wife scornfully. "Did you see any police down on the street?"

"No," said her husband.

"Not even in front of the Red Ram on the corner?"

"No," said the husband.

The woman had sat down at the table. She started to eat something, too, now, but just a little, and the whole time she listened closely to every sound that came from the street.

"I don't understand you," her husband said. "I can't imagine who would want to harm us, or why."

"I know who," the wife said.

"Other than *him* I wouldn't know of anyone," said the husband, "and *he*'s dead."

"I'm quite sure," said the wife.

She got up, cleared the table, and started to do the dishes right away, trying hard to make as little noise as possible. The husband lit a cigarette and stared at the front page of the paper, but you could tell he wasn't reading.

"We were always good to him," he said.

"That doesn't mean a thing," said the wife.

She took her stockings out of the washbowl, rinsed them, and hung them up above the radiator with pretty blue plastic clothespins.

"Do you know how they do it?" she asked.

Her husband said no, and he didn't want to know either. He wasn't afraid of those creeps. He was going to turn on the news.

"They ring the doorbell," the wife said, "but only when they know someone's home. If nobody opens up, they break the glass and force their way in with a gun in their hand."

"Stop it," the husband said. "Hellmuth is dead."

The woman took the towel off a plastic hook on the wall and dried her hands.

"I've got to tell you something," she said. "I didn't want to tell you before, but now I've simply got to. That time when the police came and got me ..."

Frightened, the husband put his paper down and looked at his wife. "Well?" he asked.

"They took me to the morgue," the woman said, and an officer started to uncover a body, but slowly, starting with the feet."

"'Are those your son's shoes?' he asked, and I said yes, those were his shoes."

"'And is this his suit?' the officer continued, and I said yes, that was his suit."

"I know," the husband said.

"'And is this his face?' the officer finally asked, removing the sheet completely, but just for a moment because the face was so messed up he thought I would faint or scream."

"Yes," I said, " that's his face."

"I know," said her husband.

The woman walked over to the table, sat down across from her husband, and put her head in her hands.

"I couldn't identify him," she said.

"Still, it could have been him," the husband said.

"Not necessarily," the wife said. "I came home and told you it was him, and that made you happy."

"We were both happy," the husband said.

"Because he wasn't our son," said the wife.

"Because he was the way he was," the husband said.

He looked at his wife's face, an eternally young, round face surrounded by wavy hair, a face that could suddenly change into that of an old woman.

"You look tired," he said, "you're nervous, we should get some sleep."

"It won't do any good," said the wife. "We haven't been able to sleep for the longest time. We only pretend to be asleep, but then we silently open our eyes, and then morning comes, and our silent eyes look at each other."

"It's probably never a good idea to adopt a child," said the husband. "We made a mistake, but now it's all right."

"I couldn't identify the body," the wife said.

"He may be dead all right," the husband said, "or maybe he left the country; maybe he's in America or Australia, far away."

At that moment another big clump of snow slid off the roof and landed on the pavement with a soft, muffled sound.

"Remember that snowy Christmas?" the wife said.

"Yes," her husband answered. "Hellmuth was seven. We bought him a toboggan. He got a lot of other gifts, too."

"But not what he wanted," the wife said.

"He went through all the gifts and searched and searched for something. Finally he calmed down and started playing with his building blocks. He built a house without windows or doors, and he put a high wall around it."

"And that spring he strangled the rabbit," the wife said.

"Let's talk about something else," the husband said. "Give me the broom, so I can tighten the handle."

"That makes too much noise," the wife said. "Do you know what they call themselves?"

"No," said the husband. "And I don't care to know. I'm either going to work on something or I'm going to bed."

"They call themselves The Judges," the wife said.

She stopped and listened. Someone was coming up the stairs. The person stopped for a moment and then walked on, slowly, all the way up to the top floor.

"You're driving me crazy," the husband said.

"When he was nine," the wife said, "he hit me for the first time. Remember?"

"Yes, I remember," the husband said. "He was kicked out of school, and you got angry at him. That was when he was sent to the home."

"He spent his vacations with us," the wife said.

"He spent his vacations with us," the husband repeated. "One Sunday I took him out to the lakes in the woods. We saw a spotted salamander. On the way home he put his hand in mine."

"The next day," the wife said, "he beat up the mayor's son and caused him to lose an eye."

"I didn't know it was the mayor's son," the husband said.

"It was really unpleasant," the wife said. "You almost lost your job."

"We were happy when the vacation was over," the husband said. He stood up, got a bottle of beer out of the refrigerator, and put a glass on the table. "Want some?" he asked.

"No, thanks," said the wife. "He didn't love us."

"He didn't love anyone," the husband said, "but he did seek shelter here one time."

"He'd run away from the home," the wife said. "He didn't know where else to go."

"The director called," the husband said. "He was pretty nice about it. 'If Hellmuth shows up,' he said, 'don't open the door. He doesn't have any money and won't be able to buy anything to eat. When the bird gets hungry, it'll return to its cage.'"

"Is that what he said?" the wife asked.

"Yes," the husband said. "He wanted to know if Hellmuth had friends in town."

"But he didn't," the wife said.

"There was a thaw then," the man said. "The snow slid off the roof, and clumps fell on the balcony."

" Like today," the wife said.

"Just like today," the husband said.

"Just like today," the wife repeated. "We had darkened the window, and we whispered, pretending not to be home. The boy came up the stairs, rang the doorbell, and knocked at the door."

"Hellmuth was not a kid anymore," the husband said. "He was fifteen years old, and we had to do what the director told us."

"We were scared," the wife said.

The husband poured himself a second glass of beer. The street noise had almost stopped, and they could hear strong gusts of wind coming across the mountain. "He knew," the wife said. "He was fifteen by then, but he stood on the stairs and cried."

"That's all over with now," the husband said, moving the tip of his middle finger between the little boats on the oilcloth again and again, without touching any of them.

"There was a gypsy woman at the police station," the wife said, "whose child lay there, run over by a car, dead. The gypsy howled like an animal."

"The voice of the blood," the husband said sarcastically. He looked unhappy.

"He did have a friend once," the wife said, "a frail little boy, the one they tied to a post in the schoolyard. They put a match to the grass around his feet, and since it was such a hot day, the grass burned."

"There we go again," the husband said.

"No," said the wife, "it wasn't Hellmuth; he wasn't even part of it. The boy was able to break loose, but he died later on. All the boys went to his funeral and scattered flowers on his grave."

"Hellmuth, too?" the husband asked.

"No, not Hellmuth," answered the wife.

"He didn't have a heart," the husband said, starting to roll his empty beer glass between his hands.

"Who knows?" the wife said.

"It's so bright in here," the man suddenly said. He stared at the fluorescent light above the stove, then he put one hand over his eyes and rubbed his closed lids.

"Where's the picture?" he asked.

"I put it in the cabinet," the wife said.

"When?" asked the husband.

"A long time ago," the wife answered.

"When exactly?" asked the husband again.

"Yesterday," the woman answered.

"Does that mean you saw him yesterday?" the husband asked.

"Yes," said the wife quickly, as if it were a load off her mind. "He was standing on the corner by the Red Ram."

"Alone?" asked the husband.

"No," said the wife, "he was with a bunch of other guys that I didn't know. They were standing around with their hands in their pockets, and they weren't talking. Then they heard something that I heard too, a long, shrill whistle, and suddenly they were all gone, as if the earth had swallowed them up."

"Did he see you?" asked the husband.

"No," answered the wife, "I was getting off the street car, and he had his back to me."

"Maybe it wasn't he," the husband said.

"I'm not quite sure," said the wife.

"The husband got up, stretched, yawned, and tapped the chair leg with his foot a couple of times.

"That's why it's crazy to adopt a child. You never know how they'll turn out."

"You never know how anyone will turn out," said the wife.

She opened the drawer a bit, rummaged through it, and put a needle and a spool of black thread on the table.

"Take off your coat," she said. "Your top button is loose."

As the husband took off his coat, he watched her try to thread the needle. It was quite bright in the kitchen, and the eye of the needle was large. But her hands trembled, and she didn't have any luck. He put his coat on the table, and the wife sat there trying again and again to thread the needle, but without success.

"Read to me," she said when she noticed he kept watching her.

"From the paper?" the husband asked.

127

"No," said the wife. "From a book."

The husband went to the living room and came back right away with a book. As he put it on the table and searched his pockets for his glasses, they both heard the cat meowing outside the window.

"Well, she's finally back, the little vagabond," said the husband, getting up and trying to raise the shutter a little, but the shutter didn't move because he had nailed the cardboard on to it.

"You'll have to take the cardboard down again," the wife said.

The husband went and got a pair of pliers and pulled the nails out of the cardboard. He raised the shutter, and the cat jumped down from the window sill. It darted around the kitchen like a coal-black shadow.

"Want me to put the cardboard back up?" the husband asked, and the wife shook her head. "Just find something to read," she said.

The husband took the cardboard with the black man on it and leaned it against the refrigerator, and the black man grinned up at him. Then he sat down and got his glasses out of their case.

"Here, kitty," he called. The cat jumped up on his lap and purred, and he ran his hand down its back and suddenly looked quite happy.

"Read me something," the wife said.

"From the beginning?" asked the husband.

"No," said the wife, "start anywhere. Open the book in the middle and start anywhere."

"But it won't make any sense," the husband said.

"Oh, it will," said the wife. "I want to know if we're guilty."

The husband put on his glasses and leafed through the book. He had simply grabbed something in the dark, and they didn't have a whole lot of books. 'But I saw him now, almost with dread,' he read slowly and laboriously, 'his regular yet prominent features, the black curls that fell on his brow, his large eyes shining with a cold flame, all this I kept seeing before me later on as if it were a painted portrait.' He read a few more words; then he put the book down on the table and said they wouldn't learn anything from that.

"No," said the wife, holding the needle up to the light with her left hand again and missing the eye with the tip of the black thread in her right hand.

"Why do you want to know, anyway?" asked her husband. "Everyone is both guilty and not guilty. There's no point in thinking about it."

"If we are guilty," said the wife, "we'll have to raise the shutter so that everyone can see we are home. We'll also have to leave the light on in the hall and unlock the front door so that no one will have any trouble getting in."

The husband made a gesture of impatience, and the cat jumped off his lap and slipped into the corner by the trash can, where a little dish of milk was waiting for it. The wife had stopped trying to thread her needle. She had put her head on the table, on her husband's coat, and it was so quiet now that all they could hear was the cat licking and lapping in its corner.

"Is that what you want?" the husband asked.

"Yes," said the wife.

"Even the front door?" the husband asked.

"Yes," the wife said.

"But you aren't really sure it was he standing there on the corner by the Red Ram," the husband protested. But he got up anyway and raised the shutter all the way up. As he did so, he noticed that all the other shutters had been lowered and that now the glow from the fluorescent light beamed out into the night like the white beacon of a lighthouse.

"It is entirely possible," he said, "that it was Hellmuth who was killed in that knifing and whose face was smashed up."

"Yes, it is possible," the wife said.

"And?" asked the husband.

"It doesn't alter things any," the wife said.

The husband went out in the hall and turned on the light, then he unlocked the front door. When he came back, his wife raised her face from the scratchy material. It had left a herring-bone pattern on her cheek, and she was smiling at him.

"Now anybody can get in," he said unhappily.

"Yes," said the wife, smiling even more lovingly than before.

"Now no one needs to go to the trouble of breaking the glass. Now they can walk right in and stand here in the kitchen with a gun in their hand."

"Yes," said the wife.

"And now what do *we* do?" asked the husband.

"We wait," said the wife.

She reached out and pulled her husband down beside her on the bench. The husband sat down and put on his coat, and the cat jumped up on his lap.

"Go ahead and turn on the radio now," the wife said. The husband reached over to the sideboard and pushed a button; the indicator light on the set shone green, and the place names on the dial lit up. There was music that was strange and that really didn't sound like music at all, and any other evening the husband could have turned the dial to the right or to the left. But tonight it was all the same to him, and he didn't move. The wife didn't move either. She had put her head on her husband's shoulder and closed her eyes. The husband, too, closed his eyes because the light blinded him and he was very tired. Crazy, he thought, here we sit in the lighthouse waiting for the murderer, and here it might not even have been our boy. Maybe our boy is dead. He noticed that his wife was about to nod off. As soon as she was sound asleep, he would get up and lower the shutter and lock the door. She hadn't slept on his shoulder for the longest time, not for years, but now she was doing just that. In fact, she was just the way she used to be, only her face had a few wrinkles; but he didn't see her face and her white hair. And since everything was the way it used to be, he couldn't bring himself to move his shoulder; after all, she might wake up, and everything would start all over again. All over again, he thought, from the beginning we wanted a child. I always wanted a child, and we weren't having any luck. That one, nurse, the little one in the third row with the curly hair, and isn't someone coming up the stairs now, a boy? Don't open the door, the director said, hush, hush. Don't even breathe. We didn't love him. The little curly-haired boy turned into a wild beast. Walk right in, gentlemen, all the doors are open, go ahead and shoot, my wife wanted it that way, and it doesn't hurt.

"It doesn't hurt," he said, already half asleep. He didn't mean to say it quite so loudly. His wife opened her eyes and smiled. Then they both slept without being aware that the cat jumped down and slipped out through the window that had been left ajar. They didn't notice that the snow was sliding off the roof, that the warm wind was rattling the window, that it was finally dawn. They slept soundly and calmly, leaning against each other. No one came to kill them; in fact, no one came at all the whole night long.

Street Lamps

Although he was not too tall and not too smart, even as a boy Hellmuth Klein wanted to accomplish something extraordinary. Not as a king or a minister but only in private, behind the scenes, and in the final analysis just for the sake of being able to say to himself: This is what I have achieved. Most likely he would not have minded working in public as well, brightly and courageously, in keeping with his first name (so foreign sounding in this country) but this seemed to be denied him from the start. In school he barely came up to the class norm. Any important assignment, any examination that had a bearing on his grade made him sick and caused him to break out in a cold sweat. A bright and courageous fellow, whose name was Leidhold of all things, was his benchmate for quite a while. Although lazy and indifferent, he was not untalented, but all the hard questions went right past him, and he simply took it for granted. One day when the teacher was surveying the rows of heads and torsos prior to asking a particularly difficult question, all the students were concentrating on their own forms of defense—indifferently leafing through their notebooks, boldly trying to hide, staring back. Hellmuth noticed that Leidhold, who had put his right hand flat on the desk, moved his index finger from right to left without looking at the teacher, all the while smiling dreamily into space. Hellmuth saw the teacher's glance directed at Leidhold, who hadn't been called on for quite a while. Then the glance was irresistibly directed toward him. He was picked. He stammered, didn't know the answer, sat down again, and watched the teacher, pale and irritated, write down a number or symbol in his grade book. Leidhold's hand was suddenly clenched; he no longer smiled, and he stared at Hellmuth almost as if he wanted to punish him.

"Whatever did you do?" Hellmuth asked as soon as the bell had rung. "He was about to have a go at you, not me; he had gotten to your name in his book."

"So?" Leidhold answered coldly.

"He couldn't do it," Hellmuth said all excited. "You did something with your fingers that forced him to go past you." And then he moved his index finger the way he had seen his neighbor do it.

"Come on, that's a joke," Leidhold said, his bright blue eyes looking into Hellmuth's, which were beginning to brim with tears in the most annoying way. But then Leidhold suddenly jumped up from his desk, on

131

which he had sat down so elegantly. He pulled Hellmuth with him through the noisy throng of boys to a room behind a partition that had been turned into a makeshift infirmary. There students sometimes managed to hide from their superiors, thereby getting out of going outside in that abominable fresh air. Leaning on a box that was obviously a first aid kit, as you could tell from its red cross on a white background, Leidhold started to explain. Hellmuth, who took the scornfully flashing blue eyes to mean suddenly awakened trust, listened attentively, as if he were about to learn the secret of his life.

"Look," said Leidhold, repeating the movement with his fingers. "Look and pay close attention to what I'm saying. You're a bit slow on the trigger. You move your finger slowly from right to left, that way you make him or any other teacher go past you, anybody at all. You just have to keep thinking: 'past, past, past'."

Hellmuth stared at him helplessly and asked: "Without looking at him?"

"Of course you don't look at him," Leidhold snapped. "I mean, that would give you away. Incidentally," he continued in a kinder vein, "the main thing is that you think only of what comes next. For example, I mean not just that the person coming into the room right now should open the window, but rather: right leg, step; left leg, step, and so on. Raise your right hand, reach for the window handle, you know. The bell already rang," he added, peering out through the split in the gray canvas curtain and nudging Hellmuth, who was paralyzed with surprise, into the hall of pushing and shoving boys on their way back from the playground. Having found his seat, Hellmuth scooted his pencil case of genuine leather over to his neighbor. It seemed a measly gift, considering what he had learned, but it was the most expensive thing he owned. Leidhold gave a short nod of thanks, and because the geography teacher up front was already telling everyone to be quiet, he bent down once more under the desk, as if he were looking for something he had dropped, and hissed from there: "Careful, this is dangerous; it strains your cranial nerves, you know." The geography lesson started, a happy pastime in front of the movie screen with its changing landscapes, which Hellmuth watched disinterestedly yet deeply moved. The landscapes led him to bold thoughts, to thoughts that went far beyond diverting a teacher's attention, and they finally started to make Hellmuth dizzy.

The reason things didn't start happening right away was that Hellmuth was a pampered little boy, careful by nature and sustained in every cautious move by his widowed mother, who was of the lower middle class. The warning that Leidhold had shared with this novice about his magic tricks achieved its full effect through the fact that the young fellow who had started it all missed school the day after the conversation at the first aid station. He died a week later, although he supposedly only had a cold. The class, unobtrusively directed by the teacher, sang something suitably sad at the graveside. Hellmuth was deeply moved. He thought he had been privy to a dying person's last secret and interpreted the strange expression in the pale blue eyes as a realization that death was at hand. He was convinced that young Leidhold had not died of a cold but of an overexertion of his cranial nerves. Thus he wavered between the wish to honor his friend's trust and the fear of sharing his fate, and many weeks went by, a short postponement, Easter itself and the Easter holidays, before he dared move his index finger for the first time while smiling dreamily as his teacher leafed through his grade book.

Actually, Hellmuth had not been idle during these weeks. He had tinkered with the experiment, with *his* experiment, theoretically so to speak, and learned that there were no limits to what one could do with this strange power. One step, one more step, sit down, hold the paper in your left hand, the right hand will pick up the pencil box, sign, right now, and what is written could be a diploma as well as a pact with the devil. Hellmuth had fantastic dreams about the various possibilities of pulling the strings. He now saw the few historical decisions he had retained from his classes in a new light. Whoever could steer the teacher's glance and intentions away from himself could do even better. At first, for instance, he could guide the hand that was about to write a number in the grade book, starting to form the scaffolding for the number 4 and then completing something entirely different: oblique upstroke, straight downstroke, the number 1. Thus still revolving around the schoolday, Hellmuth's thoughts strayed in other directions, even to the girls, who were crazy enough to sit on the park steps in the chill of the April sun, giggling stupidly. Straighten up, get up, right foot, left foot, right, left, raise your right hand, give me your hand, smile at me for all the people to see, me, stupid Hellmuth Klein who is looked down upon by everybody. Hellmuth didn't try anything of the sort yet. The start had to be made in school, with the same movement of the finger that Hellmuth naively assumed had sent his benchmate to the grave. He nevertheless carried it out, albeit trembling with excitement and without success.

"Keep your hands still," said the teacher. "Stand up, Klein, and look at me!" Hellmuth perspired, unable to answer the question that immediately followed. But he didn't take it too hard and attributed his lack of success to technical failure. He had started moving his finger too early and had guided the teacher's glance toward himself instead. He even wrote it down in his notebook in the "To Be Avoided" column while his teacher, completely unaffected, entered a very definite 4 in his.

During the following week Hellmuth repeated his experiment, and this time the teacher's glance actually did go past him. He carelessly risked his health once again that same day by controlling the cleaning lady's movements. Having stayed behind in the classroom, he silently commanded her with his "right foot, left foot, stretch out your right arm" and so on. The command was to put down her bucket near the teacher's desk, which she actually did just like that while glaring at him. Hellmuth went home in a good mood, resisting any temptation to make his mother the object of his magic during dinner. What held him back was not just a lurking headache but also the feeling that he was doing something wicked. A few days later he made an elderly woman his target, a guest of his mother's who was a real pain. He ordered her to go to the door step by step, but before leaving she turned on the spot and moved her rose-bedecked straw hat up and down like someone who isn't sure what she wants. Hellmuth was on the verge of bragging to his mother, now suddenly relieved, that he was the one who was responsible for this, but he thought better of it. After all, all plans were based on saying nothing. Any confidant endangered his ascent to a secret and mysterious power.

About this time summer was approaching. Schools were mailing letters to the parents: It will be necessary for your son to attend summer school; your son isn't doing very well. Hellmuth's mother, too, received such a letter. Hellmuth had suffered a setback that summer, especially in his written work, for which his deflecting technique could not be used. When his mother, serious and concerned, had a talk with him, he was not upset at all but pushed hard to drop out and to start working as a trainee in a bank where, once he had reached middle age, he would have altogether different possibilities of developing and perfecting his gift. Therefore, instead of going to school, he spent the next few years in a gloomy little branch of the municipal savings bank writing lists, filling out forms, and practicing his art. Resolutely but for no real reason, he would make Herr Greindl go to the window, for instance, or Fräulein Erika to the cash register. He even fixed it once so that the head clerk, whom he saw over his shoulder while he waited, wrote down the name Klein instead of his own signature, whereupon he irritatedly shook his head, looked around, and tore up the document. After such triumphs, tedious days followed. The head clerk scolded him. Fräulein Erika laughed at him scornfully instead of quietly doing her job. Hellmuth would undoubtedly have liked to touch her young, strutting bosom, but he restrained himself. If he didn't want to be slapped, the girl had to come to him, and he was not yet at that point. He wasn't actually that interested in girls. For the time being, it was exciting enough for him just to look after them when they walked by, teetering on their high heels.

He grew up during these years to the extent that he began to read the paper, even politics, which a lot of people were getting very excited about at that time. In Germany, Hitler had come to power, and he also had quite a following here. People who wore white wool knee socks were Hitler supporters. Hellmuth hated him from the very first day and considered him a rival who didn't need to practice, someone who was born with power over other human beings. Some innate sense of justice and freedom shielded him personally from this Pied Piper style that so infatuated the young people. In the same pathetic manner of speaking that he practiced in his monologues, he conversed with his great enemy, saying: Someone will emerge from the darkness and retreat into the darkness, but he will ruin you. Just how that was supposed to come about was on Hellmuth's mind day and night. There was no doubt that the Führer was out to liberate his homeland from the black-red yoke of the clerics and communists someday. It was certain that he would then march through the streets of Vienna, cheered on by his supporters. When that day came, it was essential not just to be present but to be in the front row. Still vague about the details, Hellmuth realized he would never get to that point if he didn't pretend to be a convert. Therefore he joined his colleague and former university student Allgäuer in the coffee house in the evenings, learning from him and listening angrily to his euphoria. When he went to the bank in white knee socks for the first time, he ran into Director Rosenzweig in front of the door. Rosenzweig had closed his eyes to many of Hellmuth's careless mistakes, and his old wise eyes now looked at him with concern. Like that other time at his mother's, Hellmuth came close to saying too much, but like then he refrained at the last moment. He gave an embarrassed laugh and let the director precede him, thinking only: I'll save you all, Herr Director. You'll see.

During the period that followed, Hellmuth, to his mother's utter surprise, offered quite frequently to take over the necessary jobs at the cemetery: watering, weeding, and setting out new plants on his father's grave. He performed these tasks quickly and without any thought of the dead man, whom he knew only from photographs. Because the lunch hour was short, he was barely finished before he hurried, to the amazement of the other visitors to the cemetery, toward Plot 57B on the vast grid that was the spot where young Leidhold lay, the boy who probably still had Latin vocabulary words whispered to him by the angels. Hellmuth sat down there in the damp fall leaves and later on in the snow and for his part let his young master whisper to him—in fact, this was the spot where he had his most lucid thoughts and where he ultimately got his most brilliant idea, as the first spring winds blew across the Asiatic winter wasteland of the dead.

Hellmuth went to the coffee house again that evening. Here was All-gäuer, the other trainee, but he was no longer alone. A kind of staff had formed; it couldn't be too much longer now until the Führer would invade his beloved Austria. They must prepare for war. Hellmuth insisted that an exact plan be made of where the men in the white knee socks would be posted. After all, the life of the Führer must be protected from any possible assassination attempts by the blacks and the reds. The group was assigned a place on the Ring, and with uncharacteristic energy Hellmuth urged that he himself be positioned near a lamppost, which he had in mind to climb up on. He made it a habit now to go to this ornate, old-fashioned street lamp every night all by himself and make his calculations on the basis of the passing cars. Later on in the evening he would speak silently with his adversary again, saying: A bomb? You've got to be crazy! This idiocy is going to kill you; you're headed for the insane asylum. A mad house painter, and the ones who have hailed you will sneak home in shame.

At the bank he must start practicing again, this time on his colleague Liebstöckl and on an electrician by the name of Kraus, who was temporarily working in the store room. Silently encouraged by Hellmuth, who sat there smiling with downcast eyes, Herr Liebstöckl actually unbuttoned his coat. The electrician's face contorted itself into a wild grimace. That's enough! You can't go any further without arousing suspicion! After exercises like that, Hellmuth was white as a sheet. His forehead was covered with perspiration, and Fräulein Erika would offer him aspirin. Only his mother didn't notice anything. To her way of thinking, the Alpine knee socks made her son healthier and more assertive; she took every opportunity to listen to the radio, humming "Die Fahne hoch" to herself whenever she was busy in the kitchen.

All this aside, it was almost spring, March sun, March flurries, and finally the day arrived. The Führer marched into Linz, then into Vienna. The commotion that day was tremendous. Hellmuth didn't reach his lamppost but found another one at just the right moment, and from quite far away he could hear the mad cheering, which reverberated until the black cars came into view and the raucous shouting resounded in his ears. He forced himself to remain calm, his glance seeking the odious man, the one standing there in the car with his arm outstretched. Hellmuth began his exorcism: Lower your arm, take off your jacket, throw away your cap, grimace, dance like a puppet, spit on the people. What is that madman doing? And the roaring would already turn to silence. Hellmuth's cheek pressed against the lamp's cold iron. He closed his eyes, giving instructions silently, recklessly, as the voices at his feet swelled to ugly proportions and he started to feel faint. But actually the Führer down there was already driving past, without grimacing, without dancing, without spitting on the crowd, but unflinchingly holding his arm outstretched and making a stony face. Hellmuth saw it in a flash and, exhausted, fell from the lamp-post like a pear from a tree. People helped him up, commiserated with him, and offered him refreshments. The excitement had probably been too much for the little guy; a roll, a piece of candy was put in his pocket. Feeling giddy, he finally slipped out, bought himself a pair of socks on the way, and left his white knee socks behind in the public rest room.

Hellmuth still went to the bank that afternoon. He hoped to find Director Rosenzweig there; if nothing else, he wanted him to see that he had changed socks. But the director was not in his office, nor was he to be found anywhere else, and Hellmuth was never to see him again. Like all other businesses, the deposit bank was closed because of the holiday, the desks and tables were unoccupied. Only Fräulein Erika was sitting impertinently at her typewriter staring at Hellmuth as he stumbled in through the back door like some kind of apparition. Hellmuth plopped down on his chair, thinking confusedly: Lower your arm, take off your jacket, throw away your cap, and then suddenly, come, come, come, by which he meant Fräulein Erika, the only person who happened to be around, the only person at all. Indeed, that is what he thought, come, not just right foot, left foot, reach out, touch me, but simply, come, help me, I'm at the end of my tether, I'm nothing. Fräulein Erika actually did take her fingers off the keys and came over without asking any questions or even offering him any aspirin. She was simply very much alone and extremely worried because her mother was Jewish and had already packed her bags and left. Erika didn't know where she had gone. In the meantime it was already getting dark if not exactly quiet outside. The men in the white knee socks marched past the big windows in groups, singing. The glow of their torches danced on the empty desks and on the abandoned chairs in the main office; in the distance you could hear the beating of drums. Hellmuth and Erika clung to each other like frightened children and finally embraced in despair.

Thus the two became a couple without love, even a married couple later on, who simply survived the first years of the war. They didn't have much to say to each other because they didn't have anything in common and had only drifted toward each other like flotsam on a stormy night. One time, when they took a wreath to his father's grave on All Souls Day, Hellmuth went ahead and showed his wife Plot 57B. There at Leidhold's grave he told her for the first time what he had been up to on March 11, 1938. He talked about it as if it had been a childish prank; yet he was strangely moved by it, as if the whole thing had been possible after all and as if the necessary power had simply failed him at the last moment. Erika laughed out loud in a mean way, the way some wives laugh when they have a hard time forgiving their husbands for having been a disappointment to them. Shortly thereafter she left the bank where the two of them were still working and took another job. She also left the apartment that they shared so that Hellmuth, whose mother had moved to the country now, was obliged to live like a bachelor. He took his meals in the cafeteria and spent his evenings in the coffee house: a cup of acorn coffee, newspapers, a bottle of mineral water and then another, if you don't mind, the bill please, we are closing now. Finally this lonely life slowly brought him to his senses. He realized there was nothing to be gained without some effort on his part and that it is not possible to save one's country or alter the course of history with childish dreams. Initially deferred because of poor eyesight and poor health, he soon thereafter had to take his turn. He took that despicable military oath, was sent off to the front after a short training period, and was not a bad soldier. After a few weeks in the service he was shot in the lungs by a low-flying aircraft, and he spent the last moments of his life lying on the sidewalk in a Russian city and staring through the iron scrollwork of an old-fashioned street lamp at a terribly blue sky, happy at last: Hellmuth Klein, Hellmuth Cannon Fodder, but dying for freedom because in the final analysis everyone dies for some future freedom.

Adventures of an Old Man

As if there were no more adventures in store for an old man! Most of all: to move away! But where to? Across the border! The borders are open; the children are taken care of. To find a place with a view of St. Peter's. St. Peter's is enormous, a specimen of celestial architecture hovering above the earth without any visible connection to the church. In any case, there's no real reason to go to the church since that's for tourists and beggars. To live high above it all! They put up such tall buildings these days, but there's always an elevator, and even if it's an old clunker that makes creaking noises, the cable does hold. They call the top story *attico*. It's a little house on the flat roof with terraces on three sides. If you have the money, you can put in a garden up there: roses, oleander, jasmine, like around the fountains in Palermo; they smell so sweet. Before you move, you just sell all the junk you've accumulated and keep only your most precious belongings: three shelves full of books, a length of Chinese silk with glittering suns and soaring birds on it, and a great big solid table.

You ought to have a housekeeper if you're an old man living by yourself. But the old women who take jobs working for old men are not the kind anyone would care to hire, least of all old Herr Seume who had been living for quite a few years on one of the seven hills of Rome with a view of St. Peter's. So he looked for a man who was servant and cook all wrapped up in one, and indeed he found such a man: Roberto, an arrogant young fellow who immediately put three additional persons on his master's payroll—persons whom his master never got to see except early in the morning and late at night when they hurried past, scared away like chickens. Roberto, who treated old Herr Seume's visitors with such discrimination, the arrogant, surly ones like princes and the nice, friendly ones like dirt. Roberto knew all about fine cuisine and the elegant presentation of food, except that old Herr Seume had to go on a diet soon after he moved into his heavenly quarters, not only because of his stomach, which sometimes hurt so bad, but also because of his high blood pressure, which caused him to have dizzy spells and strange fits of confusion and apprehension. As a result, the gourmet dinners that Roberto had introduced—lobster in mayonnaise and the little golden yellow *vol au vents* with the Moorish-brown, glistening chocolate cream filling and the little mound of whipped cream on top—soon stopped. A young warrior, thought Herr Seume, whenever Roberto served him, in livery that went back to his embassy days and had glittering epaulets on it like a uniform. A young warrior offering you gruel, but a soldier nevertheless, only the gruel was his weapon and a deadly one at that. For old Herr Seume didn't want to admit that his family doctor, an amiable Tyrolean who always joked with him to cheer him up, was recommending such a diet, indeed kept warning Roberto whenever he stopped by to be firm.

Roberto was to blame for everything; Roberto who flaunted his moods; Roberto who sang so beautifully out on the terrace in the evenings. But when Herr Seume asked who it was, he denied it was he. Because Herr Seume peered through the shutters once and saw a figure that looked like his servant standing out there, he thought Roberto had a twin brother who came to visit once in a while at night, to sing him to sleep; two handsome brothers, Hypnos and Thanatos, and Roberto was Thanatos, Death. Not that Herr Seume would have given that much thought to his servant all the time, but Roberto did cause him a lot of grief. Indeed Herr Seume complained to his friends about him and made up his mind to let him go and to look for someone else. But when it came right down to it, he didn't feel like it, and besides he didn't have the time.

For things were actually quite different with the issue of time, which old Herr Seume had so much of, or so it seemed to his friends. Things were bad, and they got worse every day. Time slipped through his fingers. The breakfast dishes were no sooner cleared away before Roberto would be serving lunch, and by then Herr Seume had written only a few words in fresh ink on the paper; i.e., on one of the numerous little notes that covered his enormous desk. Between breakfast and lunch there was a black hole in which the big bloomlike suns on the Chinese wall hanging slowly floated up and down; otherwise there was nothing. But then there were times when Herr Seume was awake all day, indeed fully awake. His head bent low over the paper, he couldn't stop writing, all of it flashes of original thought about the nature and behavior of people, thoughts that might have been worth printing, except that when he tried to reread what he had written in the evenings, he no longer knew what to make of it. There were times, in fact, when he didn't understand one single sentence. On those evenings, Herr Seume would walk up and down his long broad terrace examining the new shoots on his yellow roses. When a visitor showed up and praised the lovely view of the black piñons and the dome of St. Peter's, Herr Seume would point to the square down below and say: I've got to get down there. Then he would grimace nervously in that special way he had acquired lately which sometimes resembled a misplaced smile or even a devilish grin.

Now don't think for a moment that this story is going to end with our finding old Herr Seume lying crushed on the pavement down there one day. His days were numbered all right, but there was still something tucked away in those numbered days, like a piece of gold in a magic ball, an adventure that becomes visible when your days begin to wane, and they certainly did in old Herr Seume's case. There was no question of any drastic severing of life's thread. This adventure stands in complete contrast to the strict discipline and sinister nature of handsome Roberto. It was animated, curvaceous, and thoroughly feminine and had something to do with good, hearty meals and heady red wine. It started on a Sunday, when Roberto had a day off and Herr Seume suddenly made up his mind to flush the meager diet that passed for an evening meal straight down the toilet and go out to eat. He went downtown, not by taxi, mind you, but on foot to one of the outdoor restaurants nearby that enjoyed a good reputation. A young woman waited on him there and soon turned his head since she had soulful eyes and a happy, sensuous laugh. She took care of him like a daughter, like his own daughter who was living her own life far away. Beautiful Caterina, too, was living her own life and had her own problems, which she shared with Herr Seume. That occurred not right away on that first evening but on the many subsequent evenings he spent in the piñon-shaded outdoor restaurant on the pretext of having been invited out. Caterina, who had been abandoned by her lover and was helping out in her uncle's restaurant, sat down at Herr Seume's table, put the napkin in his lap, and poured out the forbidden wine, which he otherwise would have spilt, since his hands shook a little. If she was busy, she would send her little son, the love child, whose eagerness to please touched the old man and with whom he played all kinds of fantastic games the way he never had with his own grandsons. (Not until we have reached the folly of old age do we achieve a broader perspective on life!)

Caterina accepted him as man and advisor without being calculating about it. To her way of thinking he was a godsend, since he paid her bills and bought her little presents. There was no mention of Herr Seume's health except for the fleeting comment that a hearty meal and a fiery wine are always a cure for everything that ails you. Herr Seume ate hard white fennel swimming in water, noodles in spicy red sauce, liver with slivers of bacon roasted on the spit. You knew nothing about his ailments, couldn't even conceive of them. If Caterina had seen him sitting at his desk, trying hard to write all manner of nonsense, she would have had the deepest respect for him anyway. In her presence Herr Seume felt young and fit, and the strange sensations that followed such indulgences he accepted readily and almost as a sign of good health.

One evening when the pale little boy was pushing a paper boat around his plate as if it were a round island, Herr Seume got an idea that made him really happy. "Would you like to go away somewhere?" he asked. The boy stopped his little boat and stared at him dumbfounded. "On a pilgrimage?" he asked. "To Tre Scaline? To Madonna di Pompeii?" Those were the places his mother had once visited and told her son so much about, not to mention the big city of Naples and the ships that were moored in the harbor. "No, not on a pilgrimage," said Herr Seume excitedly. Privately he thought that it might be a pilgrimage after all, but a pagan one, to the Greek islands which, oddly enough, suddenly appeared and came closer on a precariously swaying sea. To go on a cruise like that with Caterina and the boy suddenly seemed unutterably desirable to him. He was already tracing the itinerary of the ship on the menu in a trembly hand and in proper zigzag lines: Thasos, Lindos, Mykonos, Santorini, Samothrace, Kos. He didn't tell Caterina about his plans yet. Not until he actually had the tickets in hand would he surprise her, and at that point he would also buy her free from the duties she had taken on.

He got up and went home where to his dismay he ran right into Roberto. Roberto glanced at him sternly and didn't go to bed later on. Instead, under all kinds of pretexts, he kept sneaking back into the room where Herr Seume was standing even at midnight, mumbling strange names to himself and looking at his servant with a glassy stare. When he was finally in bed, Herr Seume heard singing out there on the terrace once again and thought: That little stinker, he's keeping his brother here overnight. But he wasn't angry.

The next morning he took a cab to the Termini train station, where the wonderful vibration in the front hall carries the arriving passengers into the city like a strong but gentle wave, as toward an ever-familiar beach. This vibration had no affect on Herr Seume. He was simply drawn outside, so anxious was he suddenly to travel that he was jostled past his real destination, the travel agency, toward the platforms. From his high, quiet roof terrace with its pure air, he was pushed and shoved into the stinking, shouting, whirling throng of people as if transplanted from Heaven to Earth, from Death to Life. All this didn't bother him at all; in fact, there was something almost exhilarating about it as if he were being admitted to that concrete, logical world he had stayed clear of all his life.

Accidentally surrounded by a crowd of young soccer players, he nodded kindly to all sides. The nervous ticking in his face started up again and was interpreted as a playful, maybe even suggestive mannerism. Moreover, Herr Seume was immediately taken for a foreigner and teased a little. They finally asked him to sit down since, having been jostled along, they just happened to be near the wrought-iron tables and chairs by the bar. Old Herr Seume, who may have felt a bit weak at this point, actually plopped down on one of these cold little chairs, after which the young people began to wait on him in a jovially exaggerated manner in hopes of being generously treated by the wealthy American. Old Herr Seume noticed the young faces taking a liking to him. Behind them, glittering letters flashed on and off and wheels turned, and on the other side of the gate trains came and went. He heard the thunderous roar in the huge terminal and became aware of a sudden spring fragrance of flowering mimosas penetrating the odor of perspiration and cigarette smoke, of fried and baked foods. "Where is His Excellency going?" the young men wanted to know, and again Herr Seume drew in a trembly hand but full of enthusiasm the itinerary of the ship: Thasos, Lindos, Mykonos, Samothrace, Kos. In the midst of it all, he jumped up intending to go to the cash register and waving a large bill in his hand like a little banner. But a dizzy spell caused him to land between the tables and the chairs, where a couple of helpful fellows, who had run after him eager to be of service, just managed to catch him before he fell flat on his face.

There was no couch to be found anywhere close, nor was there any bench for Herr Seume to lie down on. Therefore he sat on one of the iron chairs, leaning against the bodies of the soccer players as against a living wall and slowly getting his bearings. Finally he was able to give them his address and get into a cab. A boy had picked up the large bill, settled the account, and put the exact change back in Herr Seume's pocket. Now they all waved goodbye, somewhat subdued because they suddenly realized who had paid for them: old age, maybe even death. At the last minute, one fellow jumped up on the running board, got in next to the driver, and took Herr Seume to his hill and his celestial abode. Here he was received by Roberto with such blatant mistrust that he soon got out of there. That was just fine with Herr Seume because that way Roberto would learn as little as possible about the adventure. Roberto didn't ask too many questions but got his master to bed and called the doctor. He came that night and gave strict orders for Herr Seume not to go out for an unspecified period of time.

Herr Seume was not as indignant about this as one might have assumed. For an unspecified period of time ... Oh well, Herr Seume's time was uncertain anyway, a time that scrambled morning and evening, day and night any which way and that quite frequently had Roberto's twin brother sing on the terrace in broad daylight. Roberto didn't want to admit it, of course. He looked gravely at Herr Seume and said no one was out there and no one was in the apartment; the doctor didn't allow any visitors. When the doorbell rang on several occasions, the master actually heard someone speaking quietly and animatedly at the front door, and once he thought it was Caterina who wanted to be let in. He thought he heard her voice, and now he was suddenly home again, didn't sail from one island to another with some dreamy Caterina, didn't shake butterflies out of the tree for a dreamy little son. He got up and slipped out on the terrace, which brought on another bad dizzy spell. But down there Caterina stepped out of her house; she didn't have her son with her. Very tiny and lost, a distant little figure, she stood there in the glaring noonday sun looking up, and Herr Seume leaned over the banister and moved his white head enigmatically back and forth. Then Caterina just waved quickly and fled right across the square and around the corner, no longer looking back, maybe because she was worried Herr Seume might lean over too far and lose his balance. But Herr Seume thought he had regained his balance now, his sense of up and down and of today and tomorrow. Today he would stay home and do what he was told in order to make Roberto think everything was all right. But tomorrow he would send him on an errand and then leave the house himself.

This thought put Herr Seume in such a good mood that he sat down at his desk, on which Roberto had stacked the numerous notes Herr Seume had written recently in his small, fine hand. Herr Seume picked up these notes now, reading and understanding everything. Amazed at how much clearer and bolder his thoughts were than before, he bent over the table and talked out loud to himself. Roberto found him and chased him back to bed where Herr Seume scattered his notes and fell asleep on top of them with a happy smile on his face. The next morning he remembered quite well what he had had in mind. He wrote, but not until that afternoon, a note to a friend who lived some distance away and sent Roberto off with it. Roberto left without making a fuss, but as soon as he was gone and Herr Seume tried to get dressed, it turned out that Roberto had locked the wardrobe and hidden the key or taken it with him. Herr Seume's house keys, which had their special place on the hall dresser, were missing as well. Herr Seume didn't think about giving up. Even someone like Roberto could be outfoxed, even an angel with a flaming sword. In a suitcase in the broom closet there were still some old clothes that Roberto didn't know about, specifically a very long and ancient coat that covered Herr Seume's pajamas completely and an old silly-looking Tyrolean hat that he had never been able to part with.

In his gray coat, moth-eaten by now, with his dusty little hat on his head, Herr Seume went down the stairs, indeed walked down all the many steps because he didn't have a key to the elevator. He slipped past the concierge's window; most likely he was taken for a beggar, because the concierge yelled something after him. Since Herr Seume didn't want to be recognized, he quickly, a bit too quickly, stepped out in the square where the afternoon sun glowed. He started to get dizzy again, was blinded, and walked in the wrong direction. He didn't even notice, so difficult was it for him to move, so unaccustomed was he to hearing all the loud noises.

The street led him uphill and then downhill again, along garden walls. The road should not have led downhill, and Herr Seume thought for a moment of asking, but suddenly he no longer knew what to ask and where he had actually wanted to go. A rattling taxi passed him and stopped, and the driver leaned out the window and urged him to get in. The driver was no longer looking for customers, he said, but was on his way home. The driver got a kick out of the fact that the tattered old fellow opened the back door and plopped down on the upholstered seat like a fine gentleman instead of sitting down by him in the front seat. "Where would His Lordship like to go?" he said in a mocking tone of voice. "To San Pietro?" And he treated Herr Seume like a distinguished foreigner who didn't know the first thing about the place. Herr Seume was happy to sit down. He nodded, and his face took on the old grimace, which the driver took to be their own private joke. So he kept on playing the tourist guide, announcing Porta San Pancrazio and Garibaldi, and suddenly there were little gardens with bamboo and lettuce by the side of the road. The car coasted downhill full speed now, coming to a screeching halt at the red light. Then, since the tunnel yawned like the jaws of hell to the right, he actually headed for the tall, shaded colonnades of St. Peter's.

Herr Seume reached in his pocket, but he didn't have any money. The driver took his befuddled attempts to look for it to be the last precious joke. He let Herr Seume off, leaving him standing by the fountain where the wind splashed water the color of the rainbow in his face, and the colonnades started to move, slowly but relentlessly encircling him. Herr Seume walked toward the wide stairs and staggered up a couple of the shallow steps. There stood Roberto in the coat and three-cornered hat of a guard of the church, raising his staff with ceremony. But then it wasn't really Roberto but his brother, the one who supposedly didn't exist. And now he was there after all, because he sang with a hundred voices from inside the church. A woman who came out of there slipped Herr Seume a coin, and he took it solemnly and humbly and pushed it underneath his tongue the way a child puts everything you give it in its mouth. He didn't want to go inside the church, nor did he have to. All he had to do now was let himself down slowly, on his knees, on his hands, on his face. He could stretch out on the regal steps of St. Peter's and rest until someone picked him up and carried him off, a foreign beggar, a corpse.

For Further Reading

Baus, Anita. *Standortbestimmung als Prozess. Eine Untersuchung zur Prosa von Marie Luise Kaschnitz.* Bonn: Bouvier, 1974.

Boetcher-Joeres, Ruth-Ellen. "Marie Luise Kaschnitz." *Contemporary German Fiction Writers.* Ed. Wolfgang D. Elfe and James Hardin. Dictionary of Literary Biography 69. Detroit: Gale, 1988. 174-82.

Boetcher-Joeres, Ruth-Ellen. "Mensch oder Frau? Marie Luise Kaschnitz' 'Orte' als autobiographischer Beweis eines Frauenbewußteins." *Der Deutschunterricht* 3 (1986): 77-85.

Boetcher-Joeres, Ruth-Ellen. "Records of Survival: The Autobiographical Writings of Marieluise Fleisser and Marie Luise Kaschnitz." *Faith of a (Woman) Writer.* Ed. Kessler-Harris, Alice, and William McBrien. Westport, CT.: Greenwood, 1988. 149-57.

Bostrup, Lise. "'Lange Schatten' von Marie Luise Kaschnitz als Modell eines Individuationsprozesses." *Text und Kontext* 13 (1985): 142-57.

Brinker-Gabler, Gisela, Karola Ludwig, and Angela Wöffen, eds. Lexikon deutschsprachiger Schriftstellerinnen 1800-1945. München: Deutscher Taschenbuch Verlag, 1986.

Corkhill, Alan. "Das Bild der Frauen bei Marie Luise Kaschnitz." *Acta Germanica* 16 (1983): 113-23.

Corkhill, Alan. "Marie Luise Kaschnitz' Perspective on Language and the Dilemma of Writing." *Colloquia Germanica*: 17 (1984): 98-110.

Corkhill, Alan. "Rückschau, Gegenwärtiges, und Zukunftsvision: Die Synoptik von Marie Luise Kaschnitz' dichterischer Welt." *The German Quarterly* 56 (1983): 386-95.

Elliott, Joan Louise Curl. "Character Transformation through Point of View in Selected Short Stories of Marie Luise Kaschnitz." Diss. Vanderbilt U, 1973.

Endres, Elisabeth. "Marie Luise Kaschnitz." *Neue Literatur der Frauen. Deutschsprachige Autorinnen der Gegenwart.* Ed. Heinz Puknus. München: C. H. Beck, 1980. 20-24.

Frederikssen, Elke, ed. *Women Writers of Germany, Austria, and Switzerland. An Annotated Bio-Bibliographical Guide.* Westport, CT.: Greenwood, 1989.

Gersdorff, Dagmar von. *Marie Luise Kaschnitz: Eine Biographie.* Frankfurt: Insel, 1992.

Jauker, Sigrid. "Marie Luise Kaschnitz. Monographie und Versuch einer Deutung." Diss. U of Graz, 1966.

Jost, Margot. *Deutsche Dichterinnen des zwanzigsten Jahrhunderts.* Munich: Kösel, 1968. 93-100.

Linpinsel, Elsbet. *Kaschnitz/Bibliographie.* Hamburg: Claassen, 1971.

Pracht-Fitzell, Ilse. "Marie Luise Kaschnitz: 'Schneeschmelze:' Die vier alchemischen Phasen der Individuation." *Germanic Notes* 16 (1985): 21-25.

Pulver, Elsbeth. *Marie Luise Kaschnitz.* München: C. H. Beck, 1984.

Saine, Ute Marie. "Marie Luise Kaschnitz." *An Encyclopedia of Continental Women Writers.* Ed. Katharina M. Wilson. Garland Reference Library of the Humanities 698. 2 vols. New York: Garland, 1991.

Schweikert, Uwe, ed. *Marie Luise Kaschnitz.* Suhrkamp Taschenbuch Materialien. Frankfurt: Suhrkamp, 1984.

Whissen, Anni. "Marie Luise Kaschnitz." *Encyclopedia of World Literature in the 20th Century.* 4 vols. New York: Ungar, 1981.

Translator's Philosophy:

Translating is both a skill and an art, and a successful translation strikes a proper balance between the two. The good translator strives to make the translation sound natural without misrepresenting either the author's style or message. We who translate have tough choices to make. What should we do when an accurate translation sounds like a clumsy one? Do we have the right to "improve" on an inelegant style? How free can we be with slang and idioms and figures of speech? How colloquial can we be? I think problems like these are best dealt with by approaching translation not as a reworking but as a recasting of someone else's text in a way that preserves the private bond between author and reader. And this means that ultimately (alas) the translator must strive to be invisible.

Anni Whissen
October 1994